Swan Sister

FAIRY TALES RETOLD

Edited by
ELLEN DATLOW
and **TERRI WINDLING**
Editors of *A WOLF AT THE DOOR*

Simon & Schuster Books for Young Readers
New York   London   Toronto   Sydney   Singapore

SIMON & SCHUSTER BOOKS FOR YOUNG READERS
An imprint of Simon & Schuster Children's Publishing Division
1230 Avenue of the Americas New York, New York 10020

Book design by Ann Sullivan
The text for this book is set in Hoefler Text.
Manufactured in the United States of America
2 4 6 8 10 9 7 5 3 1

Library of Congress Cataloging-in-Publication Data
Swan sister : fairy tales retold / edited by Ellen Datlow and Terri Windling.— 1st ed.
p. cm.
Contents: Greenkid / Jane Yolen—Golden fur / Midori Snyder—Chambers of the heart / Nina
Kiriki Hoffman—Little Red and the Big Bad / Will Shetterly—The Fish's story / Pat York
The Children of Tilford Fortune / Christopher Rowe—The Girl in the attic / Lois
Metzger—The Harp that sang / Gregory Frost—A life in miniature / Bruce Coville—Lupe / Kathe
Koja—Awake / Tanith Lee—Inventing Aladdin / Neil Gaiman—My swan sister / Katherine Vaz.
ISBN 0-689-84613-4
1. Fairy tales. [1. Fairy tales.] I. Datlow, Ellen. II. Windling, Terri.
PZ8.M9867 2003
[Fic]—dc21   2002030409

FIRST
EDITION

This book is dedicated to Heidi Anne Heiner—
librarian, fairy tale lover, and creator
of the SurLaLune Fairy Tale Pages Web site.

And to all the librarians
who keep young readers supplied with magic.

Contents

INTRODUCTION

BY TERRI WINDLING AND ELLEN DATLOW

When we were kids, we were told that fairy tales were only for little children—which implies, of course, that we'd lose our interest as we grew up. But we kept on reading fairy tales year after year, and they were just as wonderful as ever. Was there something wrong with us, we wondered, that we were so enchanted by nursery stories? And why, we wondered, were fairy tales considered suitable for little children anyway? Some of the stories we read in the Brothers Grimm volumes seemed grim indeed! There were queens who danced to death in red-hot shoes, wicked witches burned up in ovens, ghostly children weeping blood red tears, and wolves lurking in Granny's nightclothes.

Eventually we learned that in previous centuries fairy tales weren't considered *children's* stories—back then, they were told to everyone, young and old alike. But in the nineteenth and twentieth centuries, certain book editors, as well as the Walt Disney Studios, took hold of fairy tales and *changed* them. They turned harrowing, suspenseful stories into sweet and simple tales full of frolicking bluebirds, giggling mice, square-jawed heroes, and dumb-blonde princesses. In these new versions of fairy tales the Good were always unambiguously Good, and they always triumphed over Evil. Real life, however, is more complex than that. The old fairy tales were more complex than that too. Underneath their fanciful trappings, the old tales had a lot to say about human nature: about cruelty, vanity, greed, despair—and about the "magic" that overcomes them: kindness, compassion, generosity, faith, persistence, and courage.

Back in the seventeenth-century France there was a group of writers in Paris who loved those older, complex stories. And so they made it into a game, as they sat together in their elegant salons, to retell traditional fairy tales in clever, interesting new ways. In fact, some of the tales we love best today are versions first told in French salons, such as Charles Perrault's "Cinderella," complete with fairy godmother and rats turned into coachmen. Sometimes two writers would choose the same tale, and each would rewrite it in his or her own way—and then the other *salonnières* would decide who'd done it best. Today, three hundred years later, many of us still love playing this game—trying to discover fresh new ways to retell beloved old stories.

The authors in this book are also people who never outgrew their childhood love of fairy tales—as adults, they're still reading magical stories, and writing them too. For this collection (the sequel to our previous book *A Wolf at the Door*), we asked writers to send us brand-new stories based on older tales—fairy tales, folklore, legends, and even old folk ballads. You'll find new versions of "Bluebeard," "Rapunzel," "The Fisherman's Wife," "Tom Thumb," "Sleeping Beauty," and "The Seven Swans;" as well as two works based on *The Arabian Nights;* two different versions of "Red Riding Hood;" a story inspired by "Greenman" legends; and one Celtic folk song. Each of these authors has taken traditional material and fashioned it into something of his or her own—just as those French writers did in Paris three hundred years ago.

Who knows? Maybe three hundred years from now groups of writers will *still* be telling these stories. We hope so. Because there will always be readers who don't outgrow their love of magic.

If you'd like to know more about fairy tales, here are three good collections of them: *Spells of Enchantment* edited by Jack Zipes, *The Classic Fairy Tales* edited by Maria Tatar, and *Favorite Folktales from Around the World* edited by Jane Yolen. If you're looking for strong female heroes, try *Not One Damsel in Distress: World Folktales for Strong Girls* edited by Jane Yolen, *The Serpent Slayer and Other Stories of Strong Women* adapted by Katrin Tchana and illustrated by Trina Schart Hyman, and *Strange Things*

Sometimes Still Happen edited by Angela Carter. A fascinating book *about* fairy tales is *Touch Magic: Fantasy, Faerie and Folklore in the Literature of Childhood* by Jane Yolen. On the Internet, try these Web sites: The SurLaLune Fairy Tale Pages (www.surlalunefairytales.com) and The Endicott Studio of Mythic Arts (www.endicott-studio.com).

GREENKID

BY JANE YOLEN

We were sitting under a rowan with Dad's field glasses, Merendy and me. I was instructing her in the finer points of bird watching, which meant I was trying not to give either of us warbler neck. That's what comes when you stare up into the trees too long trying to distinguish one kind of fall warbler from another.

The woods had been exceptionally quiet for such a lovely September day. Hardly any movement in the canopy or underbrush, and it wasn't even noon, when things usually quiet down.

Above us, seen through the overlacing of tree limbs and leaves, was a slate blue sky, with clouds as flat and gray as aircraft carriers racing across.

D-Day, I thought. Or at least I hoped. *Landings ahead.*

I was thinking of Merendy, of course. Not expecting much. To be truthful, not actually knowing what to expect. My heart was hammering, though, which might have been what was scaring away the birds. *Look out, birds, boy falling in love here!* it was calling.

That's a joke. Really.

"Something moved. Over there." Merendy pointed one gorgeous pinkie in the direction of a tangle of bramble and witch hazel, because I had warned her about large movements and frightening the birds.

"Where?" I whispered. Whispering was important, and not just to keep from scaring the warblers off. I had just turned fourteen, and my voice—a late bloomer like the rest of me—had started to squeak at irregular inter-vals. It's hard enough to impress a girl who's just moved into the neighborhood if you're an eighth grader and she's in ninth, worse with a voice that sounds as if a good dose of 3 in 1 oil is not only necessary but past due. And I had to impress her fast. School started in a week, and after that someone that beautiful was going to be off-limits for the likes of me. She was high school material for sure.

"There," she whispered.

I didn't see anything where Merendy was pointing, but in our woods—deep and entwined—that doesn't mean anything. To see in the woods—to *really* see—takes a "long patience," which is how my biology teacher says a man named Buffon defined genius.

I'm not a genius in any other way, but in matters of the woods I do have a particular patient flair. To my certain knowledge we have foxes and raccoons, turkeys and deer, coyotes and an occasional bear.

I didn't know if Merendy had ever seen any of those before. She's from some kingdom or other in the east of Scotland, I think. Her father teaches at the university. He always stays in his study when I visit, calling out orders in a strange, strained language I don't understand. Merendy and her mother speak the same quick, consonant-filled tongue to one another, but a pleasantly accented and very formal English to me.

Since there are only the two houses on our little mountain and school hadn't yet started, I had Merendy all to myself. I wasn't going to ruin it with my squeaky voice.

"There," Merendy said again without a bit of annoyance in her voice.

This time I saw the movement too. I put my finger to my lips.

"Hush," I whispered.

She giggled, a sound like water over stone. And then she was still.

The forest seemed to breathe around us, a fresh woody odor. A ribbon of mist wound gently through the trees, making the sharper edges melt away.

I glanced at Merendy's profile, her straight nose, the slight pursing of her untinted lips, that glorious fall of white-gold hair. Then I looked back where the movement had been.

There! A slight tremble in a branch, but low down, so I didn't have to worry about bear.

Then the brambles and witch hazel parted, and—to my horror and surprise—a child toddled out onto the grass. A boy child.

Quite definitely a boy child.

I could tell because he was totally naked.

"Do not look!" Merendy cried out. It was not a cry of embarrassment but fear.

I stood. "Don't be silly," I said. "We have to get him back to the house. He must be freezing. And lost. And . . ."

She stood too, her back to the toddler. She stared at me with wide lake-blue eyes. "He is a Jack o' the Green, a trickster and a villain. We must leave this place. Now! While we still have the time."

"Are you out of your mind?" I told her, my voice cracking badly on the last word. "He's a baby."

But I spoke to her back, for she had already run off toward her house, that glorious white-gold hair like a wave across her shoulders.

I turned around to the little boy. "You sure better be worth it," I said, guessing that was the last I would see of Merendy except, perhaps, at the bus stop or across a crowded school cafeteria, or encircled by an admiring football team. I took five steps over to him and lifted him into my arms.

He stared at me, his eyes the light green of peeled grapes. Then he laughed, his little gums the same grape green.

Jack o' the Green Merendy had called him, whatever that meant.

Well, he was certainly a kind of green. Which definitely tipped the odd meter.

"Jack?" I said.

He laughed again and twined his little fingers in my hair.

"Ouch!" I cried, all oddnesses forgotten with the pain.

This time his laughter, high and delighted, filled the woods, and all around the birds suddenly began to sing.

I took him home, and he seemed to get heavier the longer I walked. I suppose all little kids are like that. Great big lumps of meat surrounded by charm.

Overhead warblers were wheeling and diving as if they were swallows. And a lone crow followed us from tree to tree, crying out raucously.

When I got to my house, the crow flew in front of us and landed on the lintel over the door.

If I had a strong imagination, I might have said that it cried out, "Nevermore." But it did no such thing. It just sat on the lintel and, when I pushed through the door, it decorated me with its own brand of punishment, a white splotch on the shoulder of my dad's Grateful Dead T-shirt.

The child—Jack—laughed out loud.

"Mom!" I called, and tried to dump the kid on the floor, only he clung to me leechlike and would not let go. "Help!"

The door slammed behind us, and I heard the crow flap away, cawing.

"Mom!"

She came at my call. I must have sounded really panicked. Normally her writing time is sacrosanct. Her word, not mine. It meant I had to be bleeding from an important orifice before she looked up from her keyboard.

"Good grief," she said. For a writer she had a pretty small vocabulary when it came to swears. "What are you doing with that child, Sandy?"

"Found him," I said. "Naked. In the woods."

While she took this in, she also opened her arms, and the kid—Jack I was already calling him in my mind—seemed to leap from my arms to hers.

Along the way he managed to rip my good shirt with one foot, kick over Dad's favorite Arts and Crafts jar with the other, and slobber in Mom's hair, turning a streak of it a strange green.

"You sweet thing," said Mom, oblivious to the havoc Jack had just wreaked with his one small jump through the air. "Who's your mother?"

"Mama," said Jack, and twined his arms around her neck.

"Umph!" she looked at me with dazed eyes. "He's heavier than I expected."

I wasn't surprised. He was also as large as a five-year-old. *Definitely time to put pants on that kid,* I thought. I went into my bedroom, found some boxers I used as shorts, and brought them out to the living room.

Mom was on the sofa and little Jack was on her lap. They were playing pat-a-cake, or something, their hands slapping together in a complicated rhythm that seemed much too sophisticated for such a little guy.

I came between them in the middle of one *pat* and one *cake* and managed to wrestle the pants onto him. He glared at me with his gooseberry green eyes and tugged at the pants, but could not seem to get them off, which was definitely strange since they were miles too big.

"Go away," he said.

I shrugged and turned, and the phone began to ring, which startled us both.

He screamed and put his hands over his ears.

I answered the phone.

"Do not let the Green Child into your house." It was Merendy.

"Too late," I said.

"Do not feed him. Do not tell him your name."

"Too late," I said again. "On the name thing. We haven't fed him yet."

"Your name or your nickname?"

"Oh." I thought hard. Mom had called me Sandy. But my real name is Sandor Christopher Vander. "Nick."

"Good." She hung up.

I looked over at the sofa. Mom and Jack were no longer there. Hearing giggles from the kitchen, I ran in.

Mom was stuffing Jack's mouth with Twinkies.

Twinkies? This was a sugar-free house. This was a Tofu "R" Us house. This was a We Would Be Vegans If We Didn't Like Eggs So Much house. Where in the world had the Twinkies come from?

"Mom?" I yelled.

She looked up at me with glazed eyes. Jack slipped from her grasp, now the size of at least a seven-year-old with that gappy lost-tooth look. He still was wearing the shorts, and there was a smear of cream across his lips.

"Sandy?" he said.

I felt my knees give. "Yes?" I answered.

"Cookies."

Well, I ransacked the kitchen for cookies and found a stash of Mrs. Fields. Dad must have fallen off the tofu wagon. At this point there was a sugar jar cracked open on the floor and tracks through the crunchy brown stuff. Mom's hanging herbs had been trampled through the mess. And seven free-range eggs had somehow been smashed there as well. Plus Dad's favorite flowered blue platter.

The phone rang again.

I picked it up. This time it was very heavy. I spoke into the mouthpiece. Or maybe I spoke into the earpiece.

"Too late," I said, my voice sounding like whale song, low and slow.

"No names," the phone told me.

I whale-songed back. "No."

"No names."

It was Merendy's father.

"Yes, sir," I said. "I mean no, sir. No names."

He hung up. I dropped the phone right into the egg and sugar and herbal mess.

Jack laughed at me. He was over ten years old, I bet. Mom was no longer holding him up, though she was still holding on. I felt the laughter sawing through me, cutting my cords. I collapsed on the floor.

"Jack!" I said.

"Sandy," he said back.

We were best friends. I would follow him anywhere. Idly, I ran my finger through the egg mess and then stuck the finger in my mouth. Vague thoughts of salmonella and other diseases wafted through my brain.

"Salmonella," I said. "Kissed a fella. Walking with her black umbrella." I giggled.

Mom giggled.

Jack, now a teenager, the muscle kind who would take Merendy away from me, just grinned. He deserved her, not me. He had the magic, the charm, the power. I was a nerd. A nerdlet.

"Take her," I said. "Take my girl." I was about to name her. "Take Mer . . . ," and something stopped me. Some little bit of memory.

No names.

I giggled.

"Mer . . . ," Jack said, coming over and staring at me, nose to nose. Green eyes to . . . "Got it!" He laughed and cartwheeled out our front door, going down the mountain toward Merendy's house.

The minute he was gone, I woke as if from a terrible nightmare. Saw the mess on the floor, saw Mom's stricken look. Thought about Merendy and the Jack.

"No farking way!" I shouted, and ran after him, leaving Mom to clean the place alone.

He had gone through the woods as if the paved road was too human a route for him. But it wasn't the quicker way. The road was. So we arrived at Merendy's door at the same time.

"Jack!" I roared, my voice cracking.

He turned and smiled. Definitely a high school senior. Football team. Basketball team. Track team. Class president.

"Sandy," he said, and raised a finger in warning.

"Not my name!" I cried, and head-butted him in the belly, which was clearly not what he was expecting.

He went down on his back and was about to get up, when Merendy's dad appeared at the door.

He raised his hand and spread his fingers in what looked like a Spock V, only the ring finger was flexed—which is just about impossible. I know, because I tried it later. He said something that seemed to rhyme, only not in English.

Jack's head snapped back, little black bugs streaming out of his mouth. Then he said a word that was probably a swear but in a foreign language, so who knows. And then—poof!—he was gone.

All that was left were my boxers.

"Burn them," Dr. O'Bron said. "With a branch of rowan."

"Rowan?"

"I will get it for him, Father." Merendy was suddenly at the door, looking impossibly beautiful.

"I . . . I . . ." The words stuck in my mouth. "I didn't tell him your name."

"You do not know it," said Merendy. Then she smiled to take the sting of her words away. "But I bless you for trying." She made a small sign with her fingers, and a feeling of total bliss came over me.

That was when I knew none of the seniors would have a chance with her either. That we would remain friends for as long as she stayed in our world. That I would love her till the day I died. And all that other fairy tale stuff as well.

It was enough.

JANE YOLEN, author of more than two hundred thirty books for children, young adults, and adults, has been called the "Hans Christian Andersen of America." Of this story she says, "I have had a fascination for the Greenman for many years. There are all kinds of stories about this god of the woods, who is a kind of British Pan figure. He is pictured as both a trickster and a god of vegetation. When I was in the middle of writing this story, I was in Scotland and had just visited a famous chapel that has hundreds of carvings of Greenmen. What an inspiration! But as I am an American, I decided to move him across the ocean to a place near where I live, in western Massachusetts. The actual setting is the house of my good friend, Patricia MacLachlan, author of *Sarah, Plain and Tall.*"

JANE YOLEN divides her time between homes in western Massachusetts and Scotland. Her most recent books are *Hippolyta and the Curse of the Amazons, The Bagpiper's Ghost, Wild Wings: Poems for Young People, The Firebird, Bedtime for Bunny,* and *Off We Go!,* a board book. Her Web site is www.janeyolen.com.

GOLDEN FUR

BY MIDORI SNYDER

Ⓐ

It happened once that a king went to war, and when he did, he lost first his fortune, then his crown, and last his life. But before he died, he sent his queen and infant son into hiding so that they might be spared. The queen and her son, Khan, lived alone with only two trusted servants on the edge of a great desert, where the sand shimmered golden in the sun and purple by the twilight.

"So like the palace," the queen sighed at a desert sunset, sand devils twisting into gold spires. "But see how I have faded," she said, looking at her garments that once were dyed a royal plum and now were threadbare and bleached. The queen undid the silver pins that held her hair and let the wind and sand drift through the graying silk.

Khan did not miss palace life for he scarcely knew it, and he found his riches in the desert. As a boy he hunted for the red snakes that sheltered in the cool shade of the rocks; he climbed the slender palms and retrieved handfuls of dates. He watched the hawks hunting in the distance, their wide wings spread to catch the wind. He brought home to his mother the pin scrub roses that bloomed with a sweet, dusty scent just after a rain. And in the night he marveled at the stars scattered like diamonds across the sky.

One morning the queen did not rise from her bed, and one of the servants called him to her side. "My son, I am not well, for this life in the desert without your father has grieved me more than I can say. You are almost a man now, and so I am ready at last to join him. The servants will beg you to return home, but do not, for that would be dangerous. Your father's enemy sits on the throne, and his men still search for you. You must cross the desert and find your future elsewhere." He bowed his head and she kissed him farewell. Then she sighed, turned toward the horizon, and died.

The servants wept and begged the prince to return with them to the king's land. But Khan heeded his mother's warning and could not be swayed. He gave them food for the journey, a small bag of the queen's jewels as payment, an old horse, and three blankets.

After they had left, Khan packed for himself—a skin of water from the well, dates and apricots, and seed cakes. Khan waited until the cool twilight, and then he saddled his horse. He rode into the desert, following the stars as they wheeled merrily in the sky. One star in particular attracted him, for it glowed more brightly than all the rest. He followed it until he grew weary and then, rolling in a blanket, slept beneath its watchful eye. He rose early in the morning and saw the star just before it faded with the rising sun. Setting his horse in that direction, he continued his journey.

It was on the third day that Khan arrived at the gates of a huge castle. It rose out of the desert like a giant's back tooth. The blue domes had faded to gray, and the mosaic towers had cracks. But no matter how loudly he called, there was no answer from within. Khan rode the horse around the base of the silent castle until at the back he found a patch of green grass growing near a spring. Three palms provided shade from the sun.

Khan and his horse were very thirsty after their journey, their water skin nearly empty. Man and horse alike dipped their heads into the cool water and dank. Then Khan let his horse feed on the grass while he unpacked the last of his food. He sighed at the two apricots and the half a seed cake remaining in his bag. They weren't much to fill the emptiness of his stomach. In the early twilight he looked up and saw his star trapped like a flickering moth between the castle towers. "Well," he said, "it looks as though I am here."

He was startled by a scurrying noise, and from a little hole between the rocks of the castle wall a small golden-furred creature emerged. Her whiskers quivered on either side of her pink nose. She squeezed herself through the rocks, and then, sitting on the flat stone beside him, she began to wash. Though tired, Khan delighted in the sight of the little creature. She was graceful as her tiny paws washed first her face, then scrubbed behind each shell ear; last she arched her neck to lick down her back. As she smoothed her ruffled fur, it shone in the setting sun like a spoonful of honey. She finished her cleaning, crossing her paws before her. Two black-bead eyes looked up at him.

Khan laughed, and though it was little enough for himself, he gave her his last seed cake. She took it between her paws, nibbling at the edges. And then all at once, she broke the cake in two and stuffed it into her cheeks. Khan laughed again as her small, narrow head became round and fat.

"I thank you, young lord," she squeaked. "You have a generous nature."

"Though it benefits you, small one, I fear it has done me little good," he replied sadly. "I have reached the end of my journey but am worse off than when I began."

The creature rocked back on her hind legs and wiped at the crumbs in her whiskers. "Not so," she disagreed. "In exchange for the meal you have shared with me, I shall tell you the secret of this castle. Behind these stone walls there waits a princess. It is said that she is very beautiful and wealthy, a ring on every finger."

"But why, then, does she live here? Away from everyone?" Khan asked.

"She is a prisoner of the Guardians, dangerous and long-toothed monsters," the small creature answered gravely. "But perhaps you will succeed in winning her freedom. A bride and a kingdom would be yours to gain. Are you willing to try?"

"Perhaps. What if I should fail?"

The creature *tsked* between two long front teeth. "You would die, as the others before you. But a man with a noble heart and a wise head cannot fail."

Khan leaned his back against the castle wall and considered. Above him the star twinkled brightly. "I shall try," he agreed.

"Sleep now, then. I, Golden Fur, shall watch over you and your horse."

Khan was amused at Golden Fur's offer to guard them, as small as she was. Yet when he lay down on his blanket, weary with hunger and travel, he found he could not keep his eyes open. It wasn't long before he dreamed of a woman with raven colored hair and almond-scented skin. In her black eyes, the stars gleamed.

Khan woke as the first rays of the sun slanted over the castle walls. Beside him was a tray with bread, fruit, and white cheese. Tiny etched glasses held tea spiced with mint. Golden Fur sat washing her face, her paws crisscrossing over her pink nose.

She waited until Khan had eaten his fill. Then she spoke. "Come closer."

Khan bent to listen.

"The gates will be opened to you today. Once you are

inside, the Guardians will surround you. Be brave, for they are fierce to look at, their claws like daggers, but they will not harm you as long you do not draw your sword. They will ask you to dine. Use your wits, mark where they sit." Then she yawned widely. "And now I shall sleep, for I am a night creature." She crawled into the pocket of his cloak and curled into a ball.

Khan went to the gates, and just as Golden Fur had said, they were opened to receive him. But no sooner had he set foot inside the courtyard than he was surrounded by the Guardians. There were four of them, and though they were longhaired beasts, they were richly dressed and reared back on two legs, towering over him. They had flat faces, their eyes emerald disks, and their tufted ears pricked forward from a ruff of silvery fur. They howled and hissed at him, and though their sharp teeth and gleaming claws frightened him, he did not draw his sword. They circled him, tails twitching, until, satisfied by his stillness, they sat back on their haunches and licked their terrible claws.

"Join us at our table," the largest Guardian rumbled in a deep voice.

"You honor me," Khan replied humbly.

"Well, at least this one has manners," the second Guardian whispered to the third.

"Mannered or not, they all taste the same," snarled the fourth, and a cold drop of sweat prickled down Khan's back.

They entered the Great Hall, where a fire roared in the hearth. Serving women rested on their haunches, pulling thin sheets of bread off the baking stones. Low tables were set with golden plates filled with rice, pine nuts, cinnamon, and raisins. Crystal goblets brimmed with steaming sweet tea. Silken pillows and thick carpets covered the floors. On the walls hung tapestries bearing scenes of royal hunts, the hawks flying over the scrubby forests of the desert hills.

Khan sat, being careful to note how the Guardians arranged themselves at the low tables.

"Well, my prince," rumbled the largest Guardian, "you shall cut the capon." The Guardian passed Khan a tray on which sat a whole roasted bird with plump breasts and brown crackling skin. The head was decorated with cherries and plumes of peacock feathers.

Khan carved first the head and, placing it on a golden plate, gave it to the largest Guardian, seated at the first table on his right hand. "To the father goes the head, for he must guide the family well," he murmured.

Then Khan carved the back and presented it to the Guardian with two gold earrings in the tips of her ears, seated at a smaller table to his left. Henna stained her whiskers red. "To the mother goes the back, for she shoulders the cares of her family and sees to their needs."

Next he carved the legs and passed them to a Guardian with silver-capped teeth seated to the right of the largest Guardian. "To the son go the legs, for he must run to follow his parents' commands."

Khan took the two wings and gave those to the Guardian with only one earring in the tip of her ear. "To the daughter go wings that she may fly away from her family to marriage."

"And you, my prince," rumbled the largest Guardian, "will you not eat?"

Khan was hungry, the sight of so much food enticing, but Golden Fur had warned him to keep his wits, and he knew that the food of the Guardians was not meant for mortals. He politely refused. At that the Guardians sprang up from their seats, hissing angrily and baring their sharp teeth. The servants cowered against the walls as the Guardians arched their shoulders and flattened their ears. Khan tensed, expecting the slash of those claws. But in a moment they were gone, disappearing into a cloud of blue smoke.

With them went the room's grandeur. All its rich furnishings were returned to stone. Even the wonderful food dissolved into desert plants with thick leaves and stout thorns. Brown lizards scurried along the walls where once the servants had sat.

Khan left the Great Hall, surprised to discover that outside it was already night. As he sat down by the spring the creature in his pocket stirred. She slipped out and, standing on a stone, began to wash her face.

Then she stopped, and the black eyes twinkled at him. "You have succeeded at the fist task," she said. "But now you must sleep, and I will watch over you."

Khan needed little coaxing, for he was very tired, and soon he lay fast asleep beside the spring. He dreamed again of the woman with raven hair and almond-scented skin. She spoke to him this time, and her voice was musical. She sat beside him and, in the soft breeze, her hair brushed against his face. Khan stirred and then realized it was Golden Fur's whiskers tickling his ear.

"Wake now, good prince," she said urgently. "You must prepare for the second task."

"I dreamed of the princess," Khan said, taking a piece of bread and cheese.

"And how did you find her?" asked Golden Fur.

"She's beautiful."

"Could you love her?"

"Perhaps."

"Good. Then listen again to the wisdom of your heart, and do not be swayed by the Guardians' generosity."

Khan smiled at the pretty creature, offered her his palm, into which she climbed, and then tucked her into his pocket. Khan went to the gates, and as before, they were opened to him. The Guardians appeared, and this time they were friendly, clapping their heavy paws on his shoulders in greeting. Their tails brushed against Khan's legs, sweeping the dust from his boots.

"Come," rumbled the largest Guardian. "Today you will choose a token from our treasure chamber."

The Guardians led Khan to a room, and as he entered he was nearly blinded by the light of so many jewels.

"Perhaps this never-empty chest of gold to keep your love in splendor," suggested the largest Guardian.

"Or a crown to circle her head," said the Guardian with the two earrings in her tufted ears.

"You could protect her against all enemies with this sword," exclaimed the Guardian with the silver-capped teeth. He slashed at the air with a whistling sword of polished steel.

"A gold ring for her finger," sighed the last Guardian with the one earring in her pointed ear. She dangled a ring with a smoky topaz from one claw.

Khan stared in awe at the magnificent wealth of the treasure chamber and felt sorely tempted. Never in his life had he seen such riches. Yet as he walked through the glittering room the jewels seemed cold, like shards of colored ice. He didn't touch them but did as Golden Fur bid him and waited for the wisdom of his heart to choose. He searched among the splendid jewels until at last something caught his eye. "I will take this," he said, holding up a pomegranate, its rind tough as rust-colored leather.

"Is that all?" demanded the largest Guardian.

"It is all I want," the prince replied.

The Guardians howled and spat, flames igniting in their emerald eyes. But as before, they disappeared into a cloud of blue smoke. The bright jewels became rocks, the sword a twisted stick, and the chest of gold held withered leaves. Only the pomegranate in his hand remained.

Khan left the castle and saw again that it was night. He sat by the spring, waiting for Golden Fur to wake. She wriggled free of his pocket and sat on a stone to wash her face. When she was done, she crossed her paws and sniffed the air.

"You have the pomegranate," she said. "Open it and see what is inside."

Khan pried away the leathery rind and saw that the rows of seeds were carved from chips of rubies.

"Those are tears shed by the princess," said Golden Fur.

Khan gathered them into a cloth.

"Do they not please you?" Golden Fur asked.

"I would rather be poor than gain wealth by her unhappiness," Khan sighed.

He lay down to sleep, and soon he was dreaming of the princess. Her long black hair flowed over her shoulder, and her starlit eyes captivated his heart. In his dream they walked through a flowering garden, sharing their innermost thoughts. Khan bent his head to kiss the princess, but instead of her lips he felt the soft tickling of Golden Fur's whiskers on his cheek.

"Rise, my prince, for today is the last trial."

Khan woke and saw a tray of bread and cheese. He ate sparingly and drank a small sip of the water.

"I dreamed of the princess again," he said.

"And how did you find her?"

"More beautiful than before," he replied.

"Do you love her?"

"Yes," Khan answered. "I think I do." He rose, eager to be done with the final task. "What must I do?" he asked Golden Fur.

She lowered her head, her whiskers quivering. "There is nothing I can say, for no other suitor has yet come so far."

Khan gathered Golden Fur into his palm. He smelled the sweet scent of almonds on her fur. "Don't worry, small one." He tucked her into his pocket, and with the bold courage that comes from love he strode through the castle gates.

The Guardians were there to meet him, seated on jeweled thrones. Over their shoulders they wore mantles made from golden fur. The largest Guardian, his black-tipped ears flat against his skull, rose to greet Khan.

"For your final task, my prince, we demand that you bring us one more pelt of fur to complete my mantle." The Guardian held up his cloak and showed Khan the bare spot at the hem about the size of Golden Fur's back. "Do this, and the princess and her kingdom are yours. Fail, and we will tear you apart with our claws."

Khan's blood ran cold. In his pocket Golden Fur trembled. Slowly Khan began to search the rooms of the castle, wondering what he should do. The Guardians followed close behind him, their claws clicking against the stones, their breath hot on his neck.

When he came to the last room, Khan realized it was useless to pretend any longer. He turned to the Guardians with a heavy heart. There were no other creatures with golden fur but the one hiding in his pocket, and he knew as he faced the Guardians that he would not betray her. He thought of the princess and her sad smile, and though he loved her, he hoped she would understand.

"Well?" hissed the largest Guardian.

"I cannot find the creature you seek," Khan answered simply.

"Are you sure?" asked the second Guardian. She lifted her nose and sniffed the air. "I can smell it close by," she growled.

"No," Khan said, tightening his hand on the hilt of his sword.

Without warning, Golden Fur wriggled out of his pocket. She scampered quickly across the tiled floor.

The largest Guardian drew back one huge paw, claws extended to strike. Khan threw himself between the great paw and Golden Fur. The sharp claws cut deep, scoring five crimson lines across his chest. Khan fell, the pain blinding him to all but the sight of Golden Fur trapped between the claws of the second Guardian, her earrings jingling as she ducked her head to nip at the creature beneath her paw.

"No!" Khan shouted and, despite his pain, released his sword and struck the largest Guardian in the chest as the monster pounced. To Khan's amazement his sword passed through the Guardian with ease, and the Guardian's hollow head, still snarling, rolled across the floor. Blue smoke steamed from the depths of the headless body. The Guardian with silver-capped teeth attacked Khan, and with a renewed courage Khan countered with his sword, sparks flying as the edge of his sword slid against the polished claws. But as before, Khan's sword slashed through the body of the howling Guardian, and his form split apart like the two halves of a gourd. Scorpions and centipedes rushed from the empty husk.

"Release Golden Fur," Khan shouted as he stood, his

legs trembling and weak, and faced the third Guardian. She hunched her shoulders, her fur bristled, and her twitching tail whipped up a storm of dust, blinding him. Khan raised his arm to shield his face from the driving sand and saw, just in time, the emerald disks of her eyes as she lunged for him. He slipped to the side and drove his sword into her pelt. Steam hissed and coiled in the sand, and she crumpled like old paper before his astonished eyes. The last Guardian fled the hall, but as she leaped across the threshold, she burst into flames and were quickly turned into black ash.

And then around him, as swiftly as the desert dissolves one dune into another, the castle and all its domes and towers crumbled into fine sand and was tossed into the wind.

There was no one left except himself and Golden Fur curled in a ball on the edge of a small oasis. Khan heard the anxious whinnying of his horse, and he called to the stallion not to fear. His legs were weak and he sank to his knees, the blood from his wounds staining the front of his shirt. He picked up Golden Fur gently. She lifted her small head, her black-bead eyes damp with tiny glistening tears that turned red as pomegranate seeds.

"Ah, Prince," she said, "your courage has saved me. Take us to the spring."

Moving slowly and in great pain, Khan carried Golden Fur to the spring and laid her down in the dry grass.

"Drink," instructed Golden Fur.

He cupped his hands and took a drink of water. At once the pain in his chest subsided. He could breathe easily again. The blood stopped flowing, and the gashes knitted whole until the skin of his chest was smooth and unmarked as before.

Golden Fur dipped her head, and her whiskers worried the surface of the water as her tongue lapped a drop. "Free," she said.

Her fur began to split down the back and then fall away. From within the tiny body something large struggled to get out. He stepped back as a coil of golden, rose-scented smoke rose from the small creature. The smoke cleared, and there standing before him was the woman in his dreams. She shook out her long black hair and gave a musical laugh. The stars sparkled in her dark eyes, and the wind carried the scent of almonds. She reached down and, taking the lifeless body of Golden Fur in her palms, breathed across the honey fur. Khan saw the creature stir and come to life again. She twitched her pink nose, pricked her ears, and without a word scampered from the princess's hands, disappearing into a small hole in the sand.

The princess smiled at the astonished young man. "I am the Princess Sofia. My father was once a powerful magician. He died when I was still young, and fearing that my wealth and power would endanger my life, he placed me into the little creature. He made the Guardians from paper, wheat, and water, and breathed life into them that they should protect me. Last he set the tasks, hoping that one day there might be a man worthy of my love. You were the only one generous and brave enough to help a small creature such as Golden Fur."

Khan took her hands and glanced sadly at the desert. "I have no other wealth but my love to offer you," he said. "And I fear that yours has disappeared with the desert wind."

The Princess Sofia laughed. "Love is the only wealth that matters." She turned to the barren dunes and opened wide her arms.

Around them the desert changed, becoming rolling hills of green grass. Flowers bloomed and palms sprouted from rocks, lifting graceful fronds to the blue sky. Water bubbled from the little spring and flowed into a sparkling pond and then a river. A castle shaped itself out of white clouds, the marble towers etched with flowers and calligraphy, the blue domes the color of the sky. A thick carpet of moss and ferns grew around the castle walls, while overhead doves cooed in their nests in the eaves. Falcons launched into the wind from the gold-roofed minarets.

"Look there," said the princess. "Those are my subjects returning." On a road cut into a valley of ripening wheat Khan saw wagons pulled by teams of oxen. Herd boys and farmers shouted, their dogs barking as they guided their sheep and cattle over the hills. A woman waved a bright-colored scarf in greeting. Children skipped beside a musician who marched along the road playing a fiddle as people streamed toward the castle.

Khan and the Princess Sofia were married soon after. For three days there was feasting and dancing. And so huge was the wedding cake that even now there are still crumbs of it to be found at the back of every cupboard.

❧

MIDORI SNYDER writes, "When I was a child one of my favorite books was a large, illustrated version of *The Arabian Nights.* Long before I could read, I was making up stories to go with the enchanting and sometimes terrifying images on the pages: turbaned princes flashing curved swords, almond-eyed women whispering secret advice into the ears of sleeping heroes, feathered and furred creatures, and plates of exotic foods. I also grew up in a house full of cats, and much later, when I couldn't have cats, my daughter kept golden hamsters. One day I read that hamsters originated from the Syrian deserts and, recalling my old fairy tale book, which my daughter was now reading, I imagined them as having escaped from the pages of *The Arabian Nights,* pursued by Persian cats. I wrote this story for my daughter, who likes to invent stories too, and to celebrate all the 'golden furs' who have provided us with such charming company over the years."

❧

MIDORI SNYDER is the author of the young-adult novel *Hannah's Garden* and the fantasy trilogy that includes *New Moon, Sadar's Keep,* and *Beldan's Fire.* She lives with her husband, son, and daughter in Wisconsin, where she teaches high school English.

CHAMBERS OF THE HEART

BY NINA KIRIKI HOFFMAN

My family lived next door to Bluebeard's country mansion all my life. We shared a hedge with him, and we could see the fruit-tree tops in his orchard above the hedge from our orchard.

Bluebeard lived well. All his horses were strong and elegant, his carriages beautifully appointed and maintained. His gardens flourished. Even from a distance, his house sparkled. Yet he made everyone uneasy.

I, the youngest of five children and the one most often alone, spent much of my time pushing hedge branches aside to peer between them. I saw Bluebeard in snatches; I knew that his head was bald, his brows thick and black, and that his eyes, under the shelves of his brows, held dark fire.

His beard, though, as everyone said, was a strange color of blue, lighter than lapis but not so light as the sky, more as though he had dipped it into the sky's reflection in a dark lake.

Like everyone else, I found him strange. On those rare occasions when I saw all of him, I shivered.

When I was young, my family kept our distance from Bluebeard with ease. My father, a merchant, prospered; we had friends all around us and could afford to ignore one neighbor.

After Father died, everything changed. None of us had learned Father's bookkeeping practices. Most of our money evaporated.

My three brothers joined the army. They sent some of their wages home to our mother, my older sister, Anna, and me. We had almost enough money to live on.

Mother made lace. Anna took in laundry and mending from the neighbors. And I, well, I foraged; sneaking was what I had always done best, and now I put it to use.

On my forays I observed several of Bluebeard's wives through the hedge and met two of them.

Our orchard was still bearing well when I met the first. She was chasing a small white dog, with little cries of dismay that her slippers grew wet from the dewy grasses of his garden.

I was picking cherries from one of our trees. The dog hid in my skirts.

The wife wore a hat so large it shielded not only her face but her shoulders from the summer sun. She did not want to stoop to pick up the dog, fearing paw prints on her dress, so I carried the little thing all the way back to her house and set it within the door. She did nothing to restrain it. It ran out again.

She cried.

I fetched the dog for her twice more, the last time asking her for a cord to tie it with. That was the first time I went into Bluebeard's house.

The rug in the living room showed a scene from some warmer country, where people sat outdoors and played musical instruments I had never seen nor heard, though somehow, as I leaned to look, I thought I heard an unknown song. The couches and chairs in that room were covered in cloth so soft it felt warmer and finer to the fingers than animal fur, and the colors were like flowers. Mirrors on the walls caught images of each other so that the room looked like it went on forever, framed in carved crystal. A cabinet against one wall held many small, marvelous bottles and figurines of colored stone, ivory, and pearl. The wife left me there to look. Each object was more delicate and astonishing than the last.

It was the most wonderful room I had ever seen.

Bluebeard's wife ran to the kitchen and returned with a cake sweeter than fresh cherries and laden with buttery frosting. I had never tasted anything so lovely before. The wife let me wrap most of my piece up in a kerchief to take home to Mother and Anna. She kissed my cheek and showed me out.

My hands ached with longing to hold the little wonders I had seen in the cabinet.

I met another wife in the evening, a year or so later. By that time we had had to cut down half our orchard for wood; my brothers had no wages from the army to send home, for the war had been going on so long no one was being paid.

I had become a daughter my mother had never raised me to be, one who skulked about at night, foraging for fruit from other people's orchards, beans from other people's bushes, eggs from beneath other people's chickens. My older sister held on to the rags of her dignity by taking in laundry and sewing, though the harsh soap roughened her hands. Mother was a little blind by then, or chose not to see how we put food on the table. She knitted endless pairs of stockings from wool my sister bought with laundry money and never asked where they went when she had finished them.

No one knew for sure what had happened to the wife with the little dog. Rumor said that she, like Bluebeard's other wives, had been carried off by disease—that there was something unhealthy in the air near his house, which, after all, backed on the sea marshes. Some of the villagers had seen him mourning her, his best carriage shrouded in black, the horses' heads capped with black ostrich plumes, when he rode out to take care of his business ventures. He did not bury his wives in the church cemetery. Some said he had sent her home to her family for burial.

Other rumors whispered of darker fates for Bluebeard's wives.

The new wife was pale and had a gloomy face. She was searching for herbs that bloomed at night, she said. Did I know where the Angel of Death mushroom grew?

"Is a mushroom truly an herb?" I asked her.

"Perhaps not, but it might work like one," she said. "My mind is troubled, and I want to make myself a tincture to help me sleep. The recipe comes from my godmother."

The pockets of my apron were full of apples plucked from Bluebeard's trees. I pulled the folds of my patched skirt forward to hide the bulges and led the wife into the Wastes, where high tide brought salt water so that no good crops would sprout, but one sometimes found shipwrecked things. There was a little hummock higher than the marshlands where curious things grew. I told her I had seen mushrooms there I didn't dare pick, not knowing if they were useful or deadly.

The wife gave me a strange smile, and I left her there.

It was not so long afterward that Bluebeard came to visit. My sister and I hid upstairs when Mother opened the door, for neither of us wanted to meet him; but our mother's voice was full of welcome, and presently she called up the staircase, telling us to tidy up and come down to meet the gentleman from next door.

Anna and I clutched each other's arms, then took turns dressing each other's hair and sponging spots from each other's best remaining dress. I thought of the rug I had seen in Bluebeard's house, how stepping on it had reminded me of walking on feathers.

We went down to the front parlor, the only room where we laid fires so we could work with a little warmth. Bluebeard stood before the hearth. He was tall and broad shouldered, his clothes darkest blue, his cuffed black boots shiny. Something about him made me turn my head away. I could not look at his face.

"Daughters, here is Mr. Thanos from next door, with such a wonderful offer," said Mother. She smiled. Her mouth looked stiff.

Anna and I curtsied. I fixed my gaze on the hilt of Bluebeard's cutlass. A tiny ivory moon face smiled from the pommel.

"My dears," said Bluebeard, and his voice was softer and gentler than I had imagined. "I have long admired you. I am in need of a wife. Though I hesitate to mention it, I can see that you have fallen on hard times." He glanced toward the table, where lay three withered apples from his trees in a chipped bowl, remnants of last summer's crop. "I can offer you and your mother comfort, food, and luxury. Won't one of you marry me?"

Anna and I clasped each other's hands, stared into each other's eyes. "Anna is the eldest. She most deserves the honor," I said, and my stomach soured.

"Sara is much prettier than I," said Anna. Her cheeks lost color.

I thought of the cabinet full of small stone marvels. "His house is full of wonders," I told Anna.

"Indeed," said Bluebeard. "The finest furs, the most beautiful tapestries, the most intricate carvings, paintings by the best artists in the world. My cook is skilled in the cuisines of seven countries. I have enough coal to last us through twenty winters, enough lands to raise wheat and mutton and fruit forever. My trading ventures bring me tea and spices from all over the world. The one who marries me will want for nothing."

Anna gripped my hands. I turned to stare at Bluebeard, forcing myself to study his face without flinching.

Mother could no longer see to match the colors for the stockings she knitted. We had to lay out the yarns for her. Though she didn't complain, I knew her bones ached with cold most nights; the joints of her hands were swollen and twisted. She would be so much happier if she could curl up beside a fire.

Anna looked at Mother too, then glanced toward Bluebeard. She shuddered and looked away.

"Mr. Thanos?" I said.

"My dear."

"I would be honored to accept your offer of marriage."

In the first month of our marriage I was happier than I had ever been before. Bluebeard was kind to me and let Mother and Anna visit and eat with us every day. He let me open the cabinet in the living room and take out each precious thing, delicately painted snuff bottles from

China, tiny metal, glass, and gemstone gods from distant countries with more arms and faces than humans had, cunning ivory carvings of mice and frogs and birds.

In every room of the house I found more beautiful treasures to admire. One cabinet was full of porcelain-headed dolls with human hair wigs and their velvet, lace-adorned outfits; each doll had its own wardrobe and accessories: tiny shoes that buttoned with hooks, tiny hats decorated with tinier ribbon flowers and the tips of feathers. I wondered if the wife with the dog had played with them.

I wondered what had become of her.

I hugged one of the dolls to me, stroked my hand over her blue velvet skirt. I touched her face. It was cold.

The library was full of leather-covered books with gilt-edged pages and marbled end papers. In some of them I found pressed flowers, the colors ghosts of what they had been when alive. I wondered if the herb-searching wife had left the flowers.

I did not ask those questions.

I found closets full of fancy clothes, the materials sturdier or more delicate or more beautiful than any I had seen before. The colors were rich, the fabrics sumptuous. Some clothes fit me. Some bore faint wisps of perfume from other owners. Bluebeard said I could have any of them altered to suit me. It suited me to have the warmest and the softest altered to fit Anna and Mother.

Bluebeard said that anything I found in the house was mine, one thing at a time. It became a game between us for me to search the house over and choose my favorite thing that day. The next day I would choose another, or the next hour. The house was full of marvelous treasures.

Even in the night, after we blew the lanterns out, he was kind, warm, and gentle.

I received a letter from my brothers. They said they were taking unpaid leave, as there was a lull in the battle. I readied guest rooms for them, imagining their pleasure.

Then my husband said he must travel to attend to his business. "Here are the keys to everything in the house," he said, handing me a great ring with a forest of keys on it.

"Everything?"

"Every door, every lock, every secret."

I held the ring. It was heavy with the power of opening.

"Even the dark door in the cellar?" I asked.

He took the key ring back, separated out the keys until he held a small golden one, its bow shaped like a heart. "This is the key to that door. You may open every door in my house but that one, Sara. I forbid you to open that door. If you do, you will know unending sorrow."

"What is in that room?" I whispered.

He looked away. His beard bristled. "It is the source of my strength, a chamber of my heart. It is the one thing I can never share with you."

I felt a small fire in my chest, a flare of hurt. I had married him to take care of my family, but wouldn't our marriage be better if I learned to love him? How could I love him if I could not know him?

He handed me the key ring and kissed my forehead. "I will probably be gone six weeks," he said. "Invite whomever you wish to the house, and enjoy our treasures. Order whatever you like from my warehouses; tell the cook to fix whatever you favor."

So my husband left me. Anna and Mother moved into the house with me, and we had friends from the village come for dinner. We invited musicians to perform and our neighbors to dance and play cards. The chef made wonderful confections.

I could not get the thought of that dark door out of my mind.

My husband was good to me. Could I not obey this one request of his?

But what could be in that room? What gave him his strength? What was so dear to his heart he had to hide it from everyone but himself? What was it he felt he could never share?

For four days I resisted. I made myself stay away from the cellar. There were so many other things to look at and play with. I took the gold key off the key ring and left it in the drawer beside my bed.

But every night before I fell asleep I thought of the dark door. My sleep was broken by my waking to wonder and fret.

One afternoon while Mother napped and Anna embroidered, I put the gold key in my pocket, took a candle with me, and went down to the cellar to stand before the forbidden door.

I rubbed my fingers over the key, with its heart shaped bow.

What could it hurt?

He need never know.

I would only open the door a crack, take a quick look, close it.

I could learn what it was my husband truly cherished.

I put the key into the lock.

It made such a little noise as I turned it.

I touched the doorknob.

Then I turned the key back to lock the door. Was I not happy? Did I not have everything I needed? He had asked for only this one thing. I should respect his wishes.

I took the key from the lock, dropped it into my pocket, and walked away.

I was almost to the stairs when I turned back.

What could be in that room?

What was the secret of my husband's heart?

I opened the lock, stood with my hand on the doorknob for a long moment. I listened to the house. A board creaked above me.

I swallowed and turned the knob.

I held the candle up as the door creaked slowly open.

It was dark inside, but a smell drifted from the room, warm and sweet, slightly chemical, strangely glittery in my nose. It brushed my throat with the impulse to retch. Hair prickled on the back of my neck.

I opened the door wider.

The floor was dark and gleaming. Against the

windowless walls of the room I saw long pale things.

I blinked. I put my hand over my mouth.

Could they truly be—women?

The bodies of women, their heads on the floor beside their pale forms, faces with their shuttered eyes turned toward me.

The tumbled gold curls of she who had chased her little dog into my yard. The high, troubled forehead of the one who had searched for a mushroom. And others, so many others.

My scream caught in my throat. I fumbled with the door, jerked at the knob. The key slipped from the lock and fell to the dark floor.

The floor was awash with blood.

I stooped and fished the key from the blood, my fingers horribly warm and wet and red, the worst questions rising in my mind: How could they be so fresh when some must be so long dead? How was the blood still wet?

There was a scent of magic, like flower dust, in this death-troubled air.

He had said this was a chamber of his heart and the source of his strength. What contract had my husband signed, and with whom?

I wiped the key on my skirt, pulled the door closed, and locked it.

My hem was wet with blood, and blood spotted my skirt. My fingertips were red with it. My throat ached with strangled screams. I gathered my skirt and fled up the servants' stairs to my dressing room, where I washed my hands and tried to wash my garments.

But this was no earthly blood. Its spots did not fade. I took my ruined clothes through into my bedroom, stoked the fire high, and burned what I could not clean.

I washed the little gold key. I scrubbed it with soap, and later with sand. As soon as I got the blood off one side, spots appeared on the other.

My heart was sick. I could see my future. My husband would return, and the key would betray me. He would kill me as he had all the others.

How could I live in a house that was also a tomb?

Had every other wife gone to look into that room?

I went down to my sister. "We must leave."

"Why?" She threaded her needle with green.

"I have disobeyed my husband. He will kill me."

She stared at me. Then she rose.

"You go upstairs and wake Mother," I said. "I have to pack."

Anna nodded.

I had thrown away wealth and comfort by turning a small gold key. I had found a secret I could not live with, a horror that would haunt me. We could not stay here. We would have to escape, start over somewhere else.

I took the apron with the most pockets and went downstairs to collect as many small valuable things as I could find so we could sell them and make a new start. Anna would not take things, nor would Mother. I would provide.

I had just wrapped a jade dragon in a handkerchief

when shivers traveled over my back. I turned and found my husband in the doorway of the living room.

"My business went much swifter than I thought," he said, and smiled at me. "It is already concluded, to my advantage!"

"Welcome home," I said.

"What are you doing?"

"Polishing the treasures." I unwrapped the jade dragon and set it back on the shelf.

"Did you enjoy yourself while I was gone?"

"Oh, yes, Husband." I thought of the silent women in the basement, the river of their still-warm blood.

"Where are my keys?"

I pulled the key ring from my belt. He smiled as I handed it back to him, then sorted among the keys. "But one is missing," he said.

"Oh? Perhaps I left it by my bed."

"Go and get it."

In the front hallway I paused at the foot of the stairs. Should I run now? But then I would have to leave Anna and Mother.

I ran upstairs. Anna was leading Mother down the hall. "He is home. Go down the back way," I said, "and flee as quickly as you can."

Anna's face pinched. "Come with us," she whispered.

My heart raced. I had filled some of my pockets. Surely it was better to live than go down and join the other wives in the cellar.

But Bluebeard had horses and carriages. He was huge and strong. How could we outrun him?

I stripped off my apron and handed it to my sister. "Take what's in the pockets," I whispered. "Run as fast as you can. Send help if you can, but make sure you escape above all."

"Sara." Anna gripped my arm.

"Sara," Mother murmured, her face turning as she searched for me with dim eyes.

"I must delay him! Go. Take care of Mother." I kissed each of them and pushed them toward the back stairs.

Anna hurried Mother down the hall, glanced back at me. I gestured for her to go, and finally she did.

"Wife?" Bluebeard called up the stairs.

I went to my room and got the gold key. Then I went down and gave the key to my husband.

"Why is there blood on the key?" he asked.

Cold crept into my fingers and face. I trembled. "I don't know," I whispered.

"You don't know? I know very well. You have gone into the forbidden room." His eyes narrowed. He stared at me, then said, "Oh, Sara, I hoped you would be different. I always hope they will be different, but with you, I thought we had a real chance. Were we not happy together?"

Tears fell from my eyes. I had been happy.

I had been blind.

Even now I could smell the taint of the dark-doored room below us. I could never be happy here again.

Bluebeard unsheathed his cutlass. "Prepare to join my other wives."

Sobs broke from me. "No. Please. Please don't kill me. I only wanted to know you."

"No one may know me and live. You must die."

I hugged myself. "At least give me a little time to say my prayers," I whispered.

"Very well. I will grant you ten minutes, but no more."

I raced upstairs. What if I ran down the back stairs and out the back door? Ran, and never stopped? Had Anna and Mother gotten far enough away? No! I should delay my husband if I could, give them time to escape.

My feet carried me past my chamber door, toward the back stairs. I knew the land. I knew places in the Wastes where no one else had ever been, sanctuaries I could find where others would founder. I reached the head of the stairs and looked down into my husband's face.

He stared up at me, wordless. With dragging feet I went back to my room, then crossed to the window and looked out. But there was no escape from the window except to fall two stories to the ground.

I knelt beside my bed and prayed. I glanced to the bedside table and saw the latest letter from my brothers.

My brothers!

"Are you ready yet?" Bluebeard called. "Come down now or I shall come up to you."

I rose. "Just a little while longer!" I called through the door. Then I ran to the window. I peered toward the road.

All was still.

"Wife, are you ready? Come down or I will come up!"

"Only a moment longer!" Was that a plume of dust on the road in the distance?

"Come down now!"

"I'm coming." I clutched the curtain and stared toward the road, willing my brothers to come.

Yes. It was a plume of dust. Something was cantering toward me.

"Wife. You've taken long enough!"

I heard his footsteps on the stairs. I went out to meet him. He took my arm and jerked me down the stairs, then pushed me to kneel on the cold gray stone floor in the front hall.

"A moment longer," I whispered.

"Make yourself right with God, and then be ready to join my other wives," he said.

I clasped my hands, closed my eyes, prayed that my brothers would arrive in time.

"Good-bye, Sara," said my husband. He raised his sword.

Then thundering knocks came on the door. "Open up!" The door burst open and my brothers rushed into the room.

"Who are you?" roared my husband.

"Sara! What are you doing on the ground?" Michael asked. "What is this man— Hey, fellow! Put up that sword!"

My brothers drew their swords and chased my husband away from me. Somewhere in the back of the house the chase ended. I heard my husband cry out, a bellow of anger that changed to a cry of pain, and then the last sound of a dying creature.

I hugged myself, and then I cried, for the poor sad ladies in the basement, for the life of poverty I had left without a backward look, for the pleasant life I had thought I had with my husband, for the life I would lead now that I knew nothing was safe.

I keep the gold key on a chain around my neck, but always I wear it inside my clothes. The blood is still on it, even though we have buried the dead.

Now I run my husband's businesses and sell my husband's treasures. I have provided a dowry for my sister and captains' commissions for my brothers and fine things for my mother. I live in comfort I dreamed of and craved from the day I first set foot inside Bluebeard's house.

I often find myself fingering the key.

NINA KIRIKI HOFFMAN says, "One of my writing teachers, Algis Budrys, says people read stories because they're searching for survival information.

"I never liked the story of Bluebeard. But in the wake of the September 11 tragedy, this was the tale that gripped my imagination. I wanted to write a story about someone who looked into the dark corridors of another's heart where unimaginably horrible deeds hibernated, someone who stared into that darkness, lost her innocence, and yet survived."

NINA KIRIKI HOFFMAN's books for adults include *The Thread that Binds the Bones, The Silent Strength of Stones, A Red Heart of Memories, Past the Size of Dreaming,* and *A Fistful of Sky.* Some of her stories for younger readers appeared in Bruce Coville anthologies. Viking will publish her first Young Adult book in 2003. She lives in Oregon with three cats and lots of toys.

LITTLE RED AND THE BIG BAD

BY WILL SHETTERLY

ɔ

You know I'm giving the straight and deep 'cause it's about a friend of a friend. A few weeks back, just 'cross town, a true sweet chiquita, called Red for her fave red hoodie, gets a 911 from her momma's momma. The Grams is bed-bound with a winter bug, but she's jonesing for Sesame Noodles, Hot and Sour Soup, and Kung Pao Tofu from the local Chineserie—'cept their delivery wheels broke down. So Grams is notioning if Red fetches food, they'll feast together.

Red greenlights that. Veggie Asian chow and the Grams are solid in her top ten. So Red puts on her hoodie, leaves a note for the Moms, and BMXes away.

Now, down by the corner is a fine looking beastie boy who thinks he's the Big Bad, and maybe he is. He sees Red exit the eatery with a humongous bag of munch matter and calls, "Hey, Little Red Hoodie Hottie. Got me a tasty treat?"

Red doesn't slow. She just says, "Not if you're not my Grams, and you're not."

This Big Bad wouldn't be so big or so bad if he quit easy. He smiles and follows Red to her chained-up wheels. While Red juggles dinner and digs for her bike lock key, the Bad says, "Take five? Or all ten?" and holds out both hands.

Red warms to his style and his smile—this beastie boy isn't half as smooth as he thinks he is, but half is twice as smooth as this town's seen. Red hands off the bag, the Bad peeps in, and his stomach makes a five-two Richter. He's thinking he's holding the appetizer, and Red's the main course.

Red mounts her wheels, takes back the bag, gives the Bad a gracias, and pedals off down the main drag, riding slow. She doesn't want to be a sweatpig when she gets to Grams's. The day's as sweet as a sugar donut, but Red's not happy. As she rides she calls herself a ho for flirting up a corner boy with Grams so sick. Pumping the right pedal is like pins. Pumping the left is like needles.

The sec Red rounds the corner, the Bad's off on a mountain bike, zipping 'cross town, cruising down alleys, cutting through yards, taking every shortcut he knows and making up seven new ones. 'Cause when he peeped in the chow sack, he saw the foodery's little green delivery slip spelling out Grams's name and address.

The Bad gets to Grams's front door while Red's still blocks away. He leans on the buzzer till a weak, weak voice asks, "Who's there?"

The Bad pitches his voice like Red's. "It's me, Grams! It's major munching time!"

Grams laughs and buzzes him in. She's laughing right until she sees the Bad, and then she's not laughing at all.

Red's the gladdest when she gets to Grams's place. Walking up to the door, she pokes her nose in the bag of Chinese tastiness, snorting peppers and garlic as if she were dipping her face in a spicy sauna. She has to smile. What can be wrong when a great dinner's coming?

In Grams's bedroom, the Bad thinks the same as a tap-tap comes at the door. He hops in the Grams's bed, calls, "Hurry in, my sweet surprise!" and pulls the covers up over his nose.

Red walks in the front room, saying, "You shouldn't leave your door open."

The Bad calls from the back, "It's just to let you in, my munchiliciousness."

Red heads down the hall, saying, "Your voice sounds funny."

The Bad calls, "It's just my sore throat getting sorer. It'll be better once I eat, my little main dish!"

Red brakes at the bedroom door. The place looks nice, if nice is a dark, dark cave. On the shadow that she knows is Grams's bed is a shadow that could be Grams. The shadow says, "Now, come snuggle your poor, cold Grams," and pulls the bedcovers back to invite Red in.

Red sets down the food, gives the shadow some serious squinteye, and wants to turn on every light in the room. Then she hears Grams, near to tears, add, "Or don't you love your Grams?"

Red says, "Sure do, Grams," and hops in bed without a doubt in her head. But when the Bad pulls her close, Red's a little spooked. She says, "Your eyes are way bright, Grams."

"'Cause I'm way glad to see you," says the Bad, pulling her closer.

More spooked, Red says, "Your arms are way strong, Grams."

"'Cause I'm way glad to hold you," says the Bad, pulling her closest.

And as spooked as spooked gets, Red says, "And your teeth are way sharp, Grams."

"'Cause I'm way glad to eat you," says the Bad.

Now, I could say that's when a bold cop hears Red scream, runs in faster than the Bad can bite, shoots down the Bad like the cold, cruel creature he is, finds Grams tied up safe in a closet, and Red and Grams and the cop all get the happy ever after.

Or I could say there's no scream, no handy cop, and the Bad has a happy belly glow for days, thanks to Red and her Grams.

Either way, there's uno problemo with my story: If the Bad dies, how do I know how he gets 'cross town? If Red dies, how do I know how she feels biking to Grams's?

Here's what's sure: One dies. One lives to tell the tale. And the one telling the tale is guessing 'bout the other.

Now, pick the end you like. But before you do, think on this:

The storyteller's still around. Maybe nearer than you think.

And everyone's got to eat.

WILL SHETTERLY writes, "The first version of 'Red Riding Hood' that I heard had great things: a girl goes off on a trip all alone, and a wolf tricks her into getting in bed with him. There's great dialogue: "What big teeth you have, Granny." "The better to eat you with, my dear." But it ended with a woodsman coming in from nowhere to save the girl. And I thought the point of the story was that she was too trusting. She deserved to be eaten.

"When I got older, I started reading about folktales. I learned that in the oldest recorded versions of 'Red Riding Hood,' she ends up Wolf Chow. But by that time, I was a little less bloodthirsty, and I understood why people like happy endings.

"So when I had the chance to write a story for this book, I picked 'Red Riding Hood.' Maybe because the right ending nagged at me. Maybe because it has a girl on an adventure, and a tricky wolf, and cool dialogue—"

WILL SHETTERLY is the author of *Elsewhere, Nevernever, Dogland,* and other works. He lives in Brisbee, Arizona, with his wife, Emma Bull, and their cat, Buddha. His Web site is www.player.org/pub/flash/people/will.html.

THE FISH'S STORY

BY PAT YORK

Mira was a lovely girl who lived on the edge of the great Inland Sea with her farmer father, a cranky Auntie, and her little cat, Sasha.

Mira's mama was gone. Years before, she had taken her little sailboat out to catch the great silver fish of the Inland Sea, but a great wind came up and Mama did not return, nor was her boat ever found.

The aunt came to visit after Mama was lost, and she never went home. At first she cooked and cleaned and took the eggs to the village to sell them, but as time went on she stopped working, sat with her knitting, and demanded that Mira do everything.

One day Mira was fishing for their supper from the little wooden dock that jutted into the Inland Sea. Auntie sat on the porch in front of the cottage, pretending to knit, but mostly shouting cranky and disagreeable things down the hill at Mira.

"There are no fish on that side of the dock! Move to the right where the little waves lap, or we shall all go hungry tonight." Or, "Mind your worm, girl; fish don't like soggy bait!"

Mira sighed and did as she was told. Suddenly, when her fresh bait touched the water, it was snatched by something large and heavy and bright silver.

Mira was a fine fisher. She played the fish carefully, never pulling too hard and never giving too much line, and soon the great fish was hers! She pulled it onto the dock with her net and was about to put it into her little wicker creel when the fish opened its mouth and spoke to her. "Fortunate girl, I am no mortal fish, but a magic fish! This has been a painful day for me. You are the second human to catch me. Release me now, as the old fisherman across the bay released me, and I will be forever in your debt."

Mira knew the old fisherman across the bay. He and his old wife lived in a crusty barrel that had once been used to ship vinegar. She squinted across the bay to where the vinegar barrel once stood. Now a snug cottage hugged the hills.

"Good fish, I see that you are indeed a special creature, for you have turned the old fisherman's vinegar barrel into a cottage."

The fish looked troubled and answered, "The fisherman

would have released me, from a good heart, but his wife wanted the cottage."

Mira's heart swelled with pity. "I release you with my whole heart," she said, and gently put the creature back into the dark blue waters of the Inland Sea.

The fish stood on its tail, looking very beautiful on the water. "Pretty maid," it said, "you have done kindness today; may kindness come to you."

The lazy Auntie had by now made her way to the dock, and she heard the fish speaking. She looked across the bay and spied the fisherman's new cottage. She put two and two together and realized there was a fine cottage to be had. But she was a sneak who never said what she thought, but tried to get her way with smooth or spiteful words. Instead of asking for a better house, which was what she wanted, Auntie cried out to Mira, "Don't let that magic fish go, for pity's sake. Ask it for something—if not for your own sake, think of your poor cat!"

Mira hung her head and murmured, "Little fish, I would have let you go and asked for nothing, but for little Sasha's sake, let a fish of the Inland Sea come to my line with ease so that he will eat tonight."

The skies turned blue and little yellow birds fluttered by. "You are a thoughtful mistress to your pet, Mira. It is done."

And with that the fish dove into the sea and was gone.

"Fish! You asked for fish! Look across the bay at that tidy cottage! With its porch and garden and everything just as it should be, how happy would your cat have been in that cottage! How could you be so stupid?"

But what was done was done. Auntie stomped back to the house, and Mira threw her line again into the sea. Before the bait could touch the water, a great fish took it and Mira pulled it in. It was too big for her creel, so she pulled it onto the grass, where little Sasha played with it then ate her fill and fell asleep in a patch of sunshine.

Three more times Mira put her line into the water, and three more times a great fish took the bait and was pulled to shore.

Father was pleased and astounded. "Darling child," he said, "with this fine catch we'll have food for tonight and smoked fish to last us a month!"

But Auntie was not happy at all. She brooded and brooded about the cottage across the bay. Finally she could stand it no more, and she went to Mira's little room in the attic, woke her out of a sound sleep, and said, "You thought of your little cat, and all you could think of was fish. Well, fine. But now think of your poor mother floating in the deep Inland Sea. Would she be happy to see her husband and her daughter and her dear sister living like beggars in this tiny house? Would she not want silks and jewels for those she loved? Would she not want servants by the dozens?"

Mira thought all night about her mother, and in the morning just as the sun was rising she called out to the waters of the Inland Sea,

"Magic fish, magic fish,
Listen to me,
Your friend little Mira
Wants something of thee!"

The water boiled and the air thickened and out from between the waves jumped the fish, looking at her curiously.

"You are not the first caller of my day," the fish said. "That fisherman was by this morning. His wife wasn't content with her cottage; now she wants a mansion. Look across the bay!"

Sure as her eyes were true, there across the bay where their vinegar barrel had once been and then the cottage, there now stood a great mansion of stone with a fine lawn and a great boathouse near the water's edge.

"That is a lovely mansion," Mira said, "but I have been thinking of my beloved mother, who sailed away when I was very small. Father cut a stone with her name and a prayer that she would return, but she never did. Could I have a yellow rose bush for that stone?"

"Go to your mother's stone," the fish said ever so gently. "It is done." And with a flick of its tail it was gone.

Mira went to her mother's stone up the hill from her cottage, and there, climbing over the worn surface, were the most beautiful yellow roses she had ever seen. The roses draped over the words her father had carved like a mother cradling her child.

Mira was very happy. She picked some roses and

trotted back to the house with little Sasha bouncing behind. When she saw her father and Auntie, she told them her story.

Her father took the roses with tears in his eyes and embraced his darling daughter. "You have done well, child, for nothing pleased your mother more than yellow roses. Perhaps she will smell their fragrance and so long to be home that the sea will give her back to us."

But Auntie sat in front of the house knitting and brooding over the great mansion that stood now opposite their small house, across the bay of the Inland Sea.

And when night came, she crept to poor Mira's room again and woke the girl out of a sound sleep. "You did well to think of your mother," she growled into the girl's ear, "but what of your father? He lives here in this poor, ugly house and slaves in the fields all day to grow a little grain. Does he not deserve your attention too? Why should he work so hard and long, straining himself to plant and harvest his fields, when he could be the lord of a grand mansion?" Then she left Mira, sure that her words would pain the gentle soul into wishing for a huge house and servants for her dear father.

And indeed, Mira did think of her father all night. She loved him very much. To see him working all day, bending over his hoe in the fields, was a pain and a worry to her.

So in the morning she woke up before the others and ran down to the water. There she sang out,

"Magic fish, magic fish,
Listen to me,
Your friend little Mira
Wants something of thee!"

The water boiled and the air thickened, and out from between the waves jumped the fish, looking at her even more curiously than the day before. There was a little smile on its pale fish's lips.

"You are not the first caller of my day, pretty Mira. That fisherman came again. Now his wife wants a castle and will stand for nothing less. Look across the bay!"

Sure as her eyes were true, there across the water where their vinegar barrel had once stood and then the cottage and then the mansion, now there rose a magnificent castle with soldiers on the battlements and a great flag snapping in the tower.

"That is a powerful castle," Mira said, "but I have been thinking of my darling papa, who toils over his hoe each day. Would it be too much to ask, dear fish, that his burden could be lightened with a strong horse and plow?"

"Go to your father's shed," the fish said gently. "It is done." And it lingered a bit as Mira smiled and curtsied, then with a flick of its tail it was gone.

When Papa and Auntie awakened, Mira led them to her father's farm shed, and there stood a fine, strong mare with a gleaming black mane and tail and great, heavy hooves. Leaning against the wall there was a plow, a harrow, and a heavy leather harness with shiny bells on it!

And in the back of the shed was a tidy wagon to carry their farm goods to town.

Mira's father gazed in astonishment. "What is this, my dear?"

And Mira told Papa about the fish and its wonderful gift.

"You are a good and loving daughter," said Auntie, though the words burned in her mouth. "This horse and plow will make your father's work much easier. Yet look across the bay. The fisherman and his wife have a great castle where their vinegar barrel once stood. It is a gift of the fish and could have been ours."

"But we did not need a castle," said Mira, gazing in surprise at her angry aunt. "We needed a horse and plow, so that is what I asked for."

Her lazy aunt said no more but spent the day sitting by the fire in the kitchen, knitting and watching Mira bake the bread and wash the clothes. And always her eye slid over to the window beyond which the great castle of the fisherman and his wife stood.

That night she crept up to Mira's attic and woke the tired girl up. "I have tried to help you think of others, stupid girl, but I can see it is no use. Think of your poor Auntie who came to this terrible, small shack to care for you and your lazy father after my foolish sister went gallivanting off to sea. I want a little peace, Mira. I want to be cared for and pampered. I want a life of luxury and ease, in green velvet, with blue flowers in my bodice. Do you not understand? If you cannot understand what I want, you are a cruel and stupid girl and I'll have no more to do with you."

Auntie's words cut poor Mira's heart. She thought she was a good and loving niece. Did she not catch the fish, bake the bread, and keep the house as neat as a pin? She did not understand what more her aunt could want. She thought and thought until daybreak. She went to the edge of the Inland Sea and with tears in her eyes called out,

> "Magic fish, magic fish,
> Listen to me,
> Your friend little Mira
> Wants something of thee!"

The water boiled and the air thickened, and out from between the waves jumped the fish. It gazed at her with sorrow.

"Ah, Mira, you look so sad! What has made you feel so mournful? If I had known you were unhappy, I would have come before you called, yet you would not have been the first mortal I spoke with. That foolish fisherman's wife wants to be an empress now and must have a palace. Just look!"

Sure as her eyes were true, there across the bay where the vinegar barrel had once stood and then the cottage and then the mansion and then the castle, there now stood a monstrous palace as big as a town. It had a dozen towers and many gates and armies of people in fancy dress walking in the garden. It stretched halfway around the bay, almost to the edge of her father's fields.

"That is a noble palace!" Mira said, forgetting her own sorrow for a moment. She sat down on the dock with her feet dangling in the cool water of the sea and looked at the palace for a while. The fish came closer and watched as, finally, Mira could not hide her sadness, and tears dropped into the water near it.

"Please tell me what ails you," the fish said gently, and it brushed a fin softly against her ankle.

"My Auntie came to stay with us after Mama went away," Mira said, "and she is not happy. I cook and clean and catch fish for the table, but she says that she has no peace. She says that she wants to be pampered and live in luxury and ease with a green velvet dress and blue flowers in her bodice. She says she will hate me if I cannot give her these things. But what more can I do for her, kind fish? I try so hard already!" And tears filled her eyes again, dropping now on the fish's head.

"You break my heart, gentle Mira. Will you not ask for something for your auntie? I can give her a mansion or a castle like the fisherman's."

Mira shook her head miserably. "I know better than to ask for such things. If Auntie is not happy with the sun on the water, good food on the table, people who love her, and a small cat at her feet, how will she be happy with a mansion? She will take her anger with her to her new home. She will hate everyone in the great house as she did in the small, for that is the way of the world. And that is why I cry. There is nothing at all I can wish for her that will make her happy if she is not happy now."

The fish smiled gently at Mira. "Will you trust me to grant you a wish you have not made? I think I know a way to give your aunt what she wants."

Mira nodded her head slowly, a smile of hope growing on her own lips.

"Go back to your house, Mira. I think Auntie is happy now."

Mira ran back to the little house and flew into the kitchen. Auntie's nightgown lay in a pile on the floor, and on the table stood a fine violet in a beautiful silver pot. Around the pot was a green velvet ribbon that matched the violet's green velvet leaves. Delicate blue flowers with yellow hearts grew from the center of the plant.

Mira was amazed. Her aunt was all green velvet and blue flowers. She lived in a beautiful home. She would be pampered and cared for by Mira and her father, and she would sit on the kitchen table and be admired. She was the loveliest thing in the house.

Mira shook her head. Her darling fish had done it! It had found a way for Auntie to be happy, for everyone knows that flowers don't get angry and are rarely ill-tempered.

She ran from the kitchen back to the water's edge and called for her fish.

When it came she jumped into the water and threw her arms around its gills. "You are the cleverest, kindest creature in the world. Auntie will be happy now and always with us. We will pamper and love her and enjoy her beauty."

The fish struggled out of her grip. "My own darling Mira, you must get out of the water. I long for your embrace, but it hurts me, and you will drown if you stay too long."

Mira climbed onto the dock, dripping and trembling.

The fish gazed up at her, love and longing filling its flat eyes. "You have been so kind to those you love, Mira. Do you not have any more wishes?"

"I wish I could be a fish and be with you," she said.

The fish rocked its body in the waves. "This is not a good life," it said. "Much as I love the water, it is cold, and there are so many hooks in it."

"Then, I wish you were a human and could live with my father and me," she answered.

"It is done," the fish said joyously, and in the water instead of a fish swam Mira's mama!

She climbed out of the water, laughing and crying, to embrace her darling girl.

"Ah!" Mira cried, and threw her arms around her mother's neck. Now Mama could return her embrace with all her love.

"How can this be?" Mira asked.

"When my boat broke up in the storm and I would have drowned, I was saved by a sea witch who wanted a sister for company. She promised me half her power if I would stay. My choices were few. I could agree or drown. But even then I could think only of you and your father. So I made the sea witch agree to a bargain. I would stay in the sea and share her power, but if a human asked that I become human again, it would be done. If I spoke a word of the bargain, the witch promised that I would die."

"Mother! What a hard bargain you struck!"

"It took me all this time to get away from the sea witch and find my way back to my own bay. And now because your kind heart made the request, you have your mama back to stay!"

"We are so wet! We should go to our little house and dry ourselves by the fire," Mira said.

Just then she looked behind them, across the bay, to glance once more at the fisherman's palace. It was gone! Where all the fine houses had been, there was once more only a small, crusty vinegar barrel.

"Mama! You took away the great palace of the fisherman and his wife," she exclaimed.

"Yes." Mama nodded. "The fisherman's wife wanted to control the sun and the moon. That was too much to ask, so I took it all away. They'll be happier as they are. They had better be. Now that I am human again, the powers the sea witch gave me are gone."

The two walked to the small house, and there they all live to this very day, with Father, Sasha the cat, and a beautiful violet on the kitchen table.

And sometimes the fisherman and his wife come to visit and talk about the time they were emperor and empress.

The farmer, his fisher wife, and their lovely daughter smile and say nothing.

"'The Fisherman and His Wife'" has always been one of my favorite fairy tales," admits *PAT YORK*. "I loved the notion of getting anything I asked for, and I really loved the fish! But I always wondered why the fish never said no, why anyone would want to be an empress—I had a lot of questions! So I decided to answer a few of them by writing this story. I never did figure out everything, but I had a good time trying."

PAT YORK teaches academic enrichment classes to children in first through fifth grades at Cleveland Hill Elementary School in Cheektowaga, New York. Her poem "A Faerie's Tale" was nominated for the Rhysling Award, and her story "You Wandered Off Like a Foolish Child To Break Your Heart and Mine" was nominated for the Nebula Award. She is currently working on a novel about small shopkeepers on the moon.

The Children of
Tilford Fortune

by Christopher Rowe

ॐ

It's a good world. There are good places in it like Cane County,
where the air is clearer than glass and the streams sing.
There are good fathers in the world, like Tilford Fortune.

Mr. Fortune was a farmer in Cane County. His farm
was in rocky hills, though, and rocky hills don't make for
the best farms. But he worked hard. His back was broad
and he knew the weather and he kept his children fed. He
kept their clothes mended and the house clean and warm.
He did all these things alone, because his wife had passed
away.

Strong as he was, though, one day Tilford Fortune fell
sick. He'd long dreaded the day he couldn't provide for his
three children anymore. He'd prayed that they'd be
grown, with families of their own, long before his time

came to die. But Tilford Fortune knew the weather, and he could see that a storm was coming for his family.

He called his three children to him. The oldest was a girl of twelve, tall and straight with hair the color of the sun and fine as corn silk. Her name was Sally.

"It's a good world, Sally," said Tilford Fortune, "but sad things happen everywhere. It's been hard work seeing that you children have hot food. And now I'm not going to be here any longer."

Sally began to cry because she loved her father very much. "I don't know what to do," she said. "I don't know how to plant the garden and bake the bread."

"You'll have to go out into the world, then, Sally," said Mr. Fortune. "I have very little to leave to you children, no money at all. But what I do leave to you, you must make the most of."

Sally nodded, though she couldn't stop her tears.

"Sally, I want you to take the rooster that lives in the yard. If you find a person that's never seen a rooster, then that person will give a great treasure for it. Then you can buy food for you and your brother and sister."

Tilford Fortune's middle child was his only son. He was a sturdy little boy, ten years old, his skin as brown as a walnut from playing all day long in the sun. His name was Toby, and if he didn't always like his sisters, we can forgive him.

"It's a good world, Toby," said Tilford Fortune, "but sad things happen everywhere. I've worked long into the night so that you children can have warm clothes. I won't be here to do that much longer."

Toby began to cry because he loved Tilford too. "I don't know what to do," he said. "I don't know how to sew up holes in the old clothes or make new ones, either."

"You'll have to go out into the world, then, Toby," said Mr. Fortune. "I have very little to leave to you. But what I do leave to you, you must make the most of."

Toby nodded, but still he cried and cried.

"Toby, I want you to take the scythe I use to harvest the wheat. If you find a person that's never seen a scythe, then that person will give you gold for it. Then you can buy clothes for you and your sisters."

The youngest child was a pretty little girl named Molly. She was just four and so not old enough to remember her mother. She was a lonesome child and her eyes, green as the river, were always sad.

"It's a good world, Molly," said Mr. Fortune, "but sad things happen everywhere. I've worked hard so that you children would have a safe, dry place to sleep. But I'll soon be gone."

Molly's green eyes glistened. She loved Tilford Fortune most of all, and she began to cry. "I don't know what to do," she said. "I don't know how to make new cedar shingles for the cabin roof."

"You'll have to go out into the world, then, Molly, with your brother and your sister," said Mr. Fortune. "I have very little to leave to you. But what I do leave to you, you must make the most of."

Molly nodded.

"I want you to take the cat that curls at your feet at

night. If you find a person that needs him very much, then you'll know what to do."

Then Tilford Fortune told his children that he loved them, and told them to remember his last words to each of them.

When he was gone, the children of Tilford Fortune mourned for three weeks. But at the end of three weeks, all the food in the house was gone. The shutters had come loose from the side of their old cabin, and there were holes in the elbows and knees of their worn old clothes.

Sally Fortune went out into the yard then and caught her father's old rooster. "I don't know where in the world I'll find someone who needs a rooster, but I have to go look."

Toby didn't like following after his sister, but he remembered what Tilford Fortune had said. He found the gleaming scythe wrapped in oilcloth in the barn and went to stand behind Sally in the front yard.

Molly sat on the porch for a long time, stroking her tabby cat, which was dozing in her lap. She was afraid to leave her home, but she was afraid to be left alone, too. So she put the tabby in a wicker basket and went to join her brother and sister.

The three children walked down out of the hills, then, and into the world.

As they were leaving Cane County, an old woman called out to them from the porch of her house. "Where are you children going?"

Sally was in front of the little group. "Out into the

world to find our fortune, ma'am. I'm looking for some-body who's never seen a rooster so they'll trade me a great treasure for this one."

The old woman shook her head. "You'll have to get a long way from here before you find anybody that's never seen a rooster!" she said.

And the old woman was right. The children wandered a great distance, and everywhere they went they found roosters.

They took a little boat to a hot country covered with jungles. The trees were filled with wild roosters. They were loud and colorful, with a dozen shades of green and red in their wings, and tails as long as a peacock's, but they were roosters still, and no one in that country would give Sally treasure for her father's gift.

But a man who lived there took pity on them. "Sally, Sally," he said. "Do you know what a rooster is for?"

Sally didn't understand his question, but the man wore a friendly smile so she asked him to please explain.

"No one in my country needs your rooster because roosters are for dividing time. And we know how to divide our time here. In the morning, when those wild roosters in the jungle are crying at the sun, we've already risen from our mats and gone to our labors. Some of us fish for a little while in the sea, and some of us gather fruits in the jungles. Some of us go out with our spears and hunt the fierce bears so that we have meat for our feasts. And after a while, when we have enough, we come back to our village and share what we have. We take long naps in the afternoons. At night we light fires and play music and dance. So do you know who to look for now, Sally?"

Sally took her brother and sister and went to find people who did not know how to divide their time.

After a while the children found a great building that was as polished as a mirror. It was made of metal and glass and was sealed off from the sky. The children found their way inside it to a great room divided into much smaller rooms by strange cardboard walls.

There were dozens of people there, rushing around Sally and her rooster while Toby and Molly huddled together next to a plastic tree. The people were frantic and hurried, typing on keyboards and phones, rifling through papers and printouts, paging with pagers and meeting in meetings. They flowed around Sally and her rooster like a stream flows around a limestone boulder.

Sally whispered to her rooster and set him on the gray carpet. He filled his chest with air and let out a loud COCK-A-DOODLE-DOO!

And the people stopped. They all turned to stare and didn't even notice that their beepers were beeping and their faxes were faxing. A dark-haired woman who might have been beautiful if she hadn't looked so tired and worried leaned forward and said, "Little girl, why have you brought that bird into our office?"

Sally said, "To trade him for a great treasure."

The people all laughed, and some of them started shuffling away, blinking in the bright white electric light.

But the dark-haired woman said, "Why would we need a rooster, little girl?"

Sally said, "To show you how to divide your time."

The lady said, "But we know how to do that. See here? My watch shows me the time in Tokyo and Tripoli. My calendar has my days sliced into hours and my hours sliced into minutes. Our big white board has our meetings written out weeks in advance!" All the people nodded because what the lady said was true. They all had watches and calendars as advanced as the dark-haired woman's.

"I don't know what time it is in Tripoli, it's true," said Sally. "And this rooster has never been to Tokyo. But listen here. At every sunrise, he lets out a cry. If you're sleeping, when you hear him you know it's time to rise up. Then you can go out and do your work for a little while. When you have enough, you can all gather together and share what you've made or found or gathered. You can take naps in the afternoons, and at night you can build bonfires and dance."

The people there hadn't taken naps in the afternoons for a very long time. The beautiful lady—and she *was* beautiful, just very tired—took off her gold watch and gave it to Sally. "I could use a nap," she said.

A pale man dropped his great pile of papers to the floor and took a pager from his pocket. He put it in a pile with his portable phone and his car alarm deactivator. "I haven't been dancing since I got this job," he said.

And all the rest of the people there put *their* watches in a pile at Sally's feet. They took the rooster and sat him on top of the watercooler, and then they knew how to divide their time.

Toby looked at all the gold watches that Sally brought out of the sad building, and they made him feel a little more hopeful. He'd been afraid he'd never find anyone who hadn't seen a scythe, but if Sally had found people who'd never seen a rooster, then he could find people who needed the scythe his father had left him.

He lifted his chin because now it was his turn to do the looking. He led his sisters out across the wide world.

And lost his hope. For no matter where they went, no matter how many people he asked, Toby could find no one who marveled at his scythe.

Finally, they came to a misty island full of mountains and gardens. The houses were made out of paper there, and the people wore long silk jackets. The paths around the houses were kept clear of high grass by people swinging scythes much like Toby's. No one in that country would give him gold for his father's gift.

A lady there saw the children, and Toby looked so sad that she took pity on him. "Toby, Toby," she said. "Do you know what a scythe is for?"

Toby didn't understand the question, but the lady was very kind and explained.

"No one on my island needs your scythe because scythes are for clearing a space in the green earth. And we've all found a peaceful place among the trees and grasses. We plant our gardens where good things were already growing. We place our houses among the trees in clearings that the trees have left for us. Look at the brook there, and watch the old carp rise up to chase the dragonfly. We live in the land like he lives in the water, letting it flow where it will, and following the current of the blooms and birds. So do you know who to look for now, Toby?"

Toby took his sisters to find people who didn't have a peaceful place in the earth.

They heard the subdivision before they saw it. The great roar and clash of motors and spinning blades could be heard for miles around. And when they *did* finally come to the great brick wall around the brand-new neighborhood, they saw towering clouds of smelly blue smoke rising into the sky.

The development had a black iron gate across the street leading into it, but the children were small and slipped between the bars. All around them they saw huge houses on small yards. The houses all looked alike, and all of the yards were swarming with people.

There were men roaring around on giant lawn tractors and women blowing grass and leaves with grass and leaf blowers. They were using hedge trimmers with engines to square all the hedges and buzzing weed whackers to whack all the weeds.

Toby unwrapped the scythe from its oilcloth and walked into the middle of the street. The sunlight caught its keen edge, and the sounds of the engines died away until all was quiet. Not even a bird called because there were no trees in the subdivision for birds to rest on.

A sunburnt man set down his electric shears and said,

"Little boy, why have you brought that old hand tool into our gated community?"

Toby said, "To trade it for gold."

The people all laughed, and some of them started to turn back to the dry little lawns they'd been grooming. But the sunburnt man said, "Why would we need a scythe, little boy?"

Toby said, "To clear a place in the green earth."

The man said, "But we know how to do that. See all these machines? I can clear my lawn of unauthorized weeds in five minutes flat with my four speed lawn mower. Our vines never grow where we don't want them to because we spray them with poison spray. Our flowers stay in their tidy white boxes, and this whole subdivision is clear, clear, clear!" All the people nodded. They patted their machines but then hissed and sucked their fingers because the engines were still hot.

"This scythe wouldn't be much for taming vines, that's true," said Toby. "And you'd have to let your flowers grow out of their boxes if this was the tool you used. But see here. When you let the blooms bloom and the trees grow, you'll make a peaceful place on the earth. You can sit quiet in the shade and hear the birds sing. When the vine flows across the path, you can flow around it and have a little peace in the world."

Peace and quiet were hard to find in the subdivision. The sunburnt man thought a minute, then dug a big gold coin out of his pocket and gave it to Toby. "I haven't heard a bird sing for a long time."

A woman pulled off her gardening gloves and found another coin for Toby. She put it on the street next to Tilford Fortune's old scythe. "I'd like a little peace with the earth; I'd like the earth to feel at peace with me."

And all the rest of the people gave Toby coins or gold necklaces. They put the loud, smoking machines away and let the plants and animals come back to live among them.

When the children had walked a little way from the subdivision, little Molly sat down on the ground and started to cry. She hugged the wicker basket she'd carried on all their journeying in her lap.

"Don't cry, Molly," said Sally. "We'll find a man who's never seen a cat. Or at least we'll find out what a cat is for and take it to people who need it."

But Molly cried still.

"Don't worry, Molly," said Toby. "We didn't think we'd find out what roosters or scythes are for, but we did."

Little Molly shook her head. "I *know* what cats are for," she said. "Cats are for holding in your lap when you're sad or lonesome. I'm sad now, so I'm holding this cat here."

The lid of the wicker basket popped open, and the big yellow cat stretched out. He looked up into Molly's green eyes and started kneading her stomach. He purred and purred.

"But why are you sad, Molly?" asked Sally and Toby.

"I'm sad because we have to sell our cat," Molly said. "With all the watches you'll trade for food, and with all the gold you'll buy new clothes. I know we need a new house, but I love our kitty."

Then Sally and Toby were sad too because they loved the cat as much as Molly did. So they sat on the ground, and the cat went around from lap to lap, purring.

Finally, Sally stood up. She said, "We're being silly. There are plenty of watches and coins to buy food and clothes *and* a new house."

Toby said, "But our father told us to take the things he gave us and trade them for treasure."

Molly thought about the last thing her father had told her. "No, Toby. He said to find someone who needs a cat, and that I would know what to do then."

Sally asked her, "Have you found someone who needs a cat?"

Molly nodded. "We do," she said.

Then Toby asked her, "Do you know what to do now?"

Molly nodded again.

Then she stood up and put the tabby back in its basket, and she led her brother and sister home.

They traded the watches and the coins for food and clothes, and their neighbors came and helped them fix the shingles and the shutters on their cabin. In the mornings they woke up and went out and did their work for a little while. In the afternoons they rested among the wildflowers that Tilford Fortune had always let grow right up against the walls. And at night they lit bonfires and danced.

"Like Sally, Toby, and Molly," says *CHRISTOPHER ROWE*, "I live in a rural county in Kentucky. Like them, I once had to leave—and when I did, I had to work in offices and live in neighborhoods like the ones the children of Tilford Fortune visit in this story. I'm glad I found my way home."

CHRISTOPHER ROWE writes a column for a magazine based in his hometown, stories for books and magazines, and is working on his first novel. When he's not writing, he spends as much time tramping about in the woods as possible and working on the farm his family has owned for three generations, which also employs (at last count) 291 cows, thirty-one cats, and one little dog.

The Girl in the Attic

by Lois Metzger

Sitting on a small wooden bench, Ava could see the blue sky turn orange through the tiny attic window. The air smelled good, like wet leaves, and birds chattered as they always did in the early evening. She could hear her stepmother, too, tearing at weeds in the garden, cursing them for their very existence, despite her best efforts with pesticides and poisons. But Ava liked the weeds—tall and green, they looked good enough to eat.

She went to an all-girls' school, and that morning her stepmother had spoken to the school psychologist.

"She won't talk," her stepmother said to Dr. Fran Munder while Ava waited in the hall. The door was open a crack; she could hear everything.

"I've consulted with her teachers," Dr. Munder said.

"They say Ava talks, maybe not excessively, but when necessary. She's a good student. Maybe she doesn't have close friends, but the other girls don't shun her either—"

"You don't get it," her stepmother said. "She won't talk to *me*. I try—I really try. I think I've done quite well, under the circumstances. Ever since her father died—oh, never mind!"

"No, please." Dr. Munder spoke gently. "Go on."

"Well. He died several months ago. Sudden illness. A little cough—you think it's nothing. Well. It wasn't nothing."

"How frightening. I have a little cough myself."

"We'd only been married a short time. Whirlwind romance, very passionate, you understand?"

Dr. Munder coughed. "I wonder . . . Maybe I'll see the school nurse. This cough. Just in case."

"I didn't have children—never wanted them, frankly— but when Ava came with the package, so to speak, I was pleased. We didn't click right away, but I figured, give it time. Well, I tried—I tried hard. I got her a new wardrobe. Oh, I know she has to wear a uniform to school, but I got her beautiful weekend clothes and barrettes for her hair. She has very long hair—I saw her come out of the shower— it's down below her waist. Did you know that?"

"No," Dr. Munder said. "We ask that our girls wear their hair off their faces, off their necks."

"But she wears her hair like that at home, too—even at night! Does she ever wear anything I got for her? No. She had this old blanket, practically in shreds. Now she has a down quilt. I've created a dream-come-true bedroom for her, with a canopy bed and lace curtains. Does she spend any time there? No. She sits in the *attic*—that musty old place!"

"Perhaps she misses her real mother."

"She was only an infant when her real mother died. Her poor father had to raise her all by himself. That was why he was so happy, so grateful for me. He and his daughter were very close, but when the girl turned thirteen last year, he felt she needed a woman to talk to. Well. If he only knew!"

Ava was summoned to the room. Dr. Munder had fluffy hair you could see through. Ava sat in a wooden chair next to her stepmother, who adjusted herself in a swivel chair, crossing her long, slender legs at the ankles.

"Ava, is this true, that you won't talk to your stepmother?" Dr. Munder asked.

Ava shrugged.

"You see? You see?" Ava's stepmother was a beautiful woman, even in anger, with high, chiseled cheekbones and large, dark eyes.

Ava, in the attic, watched the sun dip below the tree line. Sparrows and blue jays and even a cardinal flew by, from branch to leafy branch. She liked sparrows because they looked sturdy, and she liked blue jays, too, even their harsh voices. Cardinals, with their shocking redness, might be the most beautiful of all.

But that day a different bird showed up and sat right

on the windowsill. It wasn't much to look at. It was little and round, and had a light brown breast with dark streaks of brown, and darker wings with even darker streaks of brown. It tilted its head at her, stared at her with eyes that were bright and alert.

"Little brown bird," she heard herself say. "Are you hungry?"

The bird looked at the windowsill and flew away.

She ran downstairs to the kitchen, got a slice of bread, and came back to the attic. She tore apart the bread and placed several small pieces on the windowsill.

The little brown bird came back. It ate the pieces of bread and then stared at her.

"More?"

The bird flew away again.

This time she got several slices of bread. Lined up the pieces, and waited. But the bird didn't come back. She put the bread away in a plastic bag.

That night she looked up the bird in one of her father's books—all she had left of him, except for a few photographs. He'd been a bird-watcher and for years belonged to a group that went outside in the early hours with mosquito nets and binoculars. So. It was a house finch—female, because the males had a bright red forehead. So. The bird was a *she*.

The next afternoon Ava sat at the windowsill with the pieces of bread all lined up and ready. It was a beautiful fall day, cool and glowing.

The little brown bird came back.

"Hello! Are you hungry?"

The bird ate every piece. This time she didn't fly away, but sat there looking at Ava.

"More?"

"No," the bird said.

Well.

"Are you really talking?" Ava said, "or am I crazy?"

"I don't have time for this," the bird said, and flew away.

By dinnertime, Ava had convinced herself she had imagined the whole thing—including the tiny bird's surprisingly deep, vibrant voice. As always, she ate in silence, cleared the table, loaded up the dishwasher.

"Honestly, Ava," her stepmother said. "He was my best friend too! You're not the only one who wishes . . . wishes for something she can't have."

Ava went to her room. She slept in a sleeping bag on top of her mattress. She didn't like the new puffy quilt—it was too soft, too warm. She missed her old blue cotton blanket. And that new paisley wallpaper . . . it hurt her eyes to look at it.

The next day she went to the attic, spread out the bread. The bird came, and ate, and stared at her.

"All right, maybe I'm not crazy," Ava said. "Maybe you can talk."

"I can talk. Maybe not excessively, but when necessary."

That sounded familiar.

"You don't understand," the bird said. "Every time, they have to convince themselves they're not crazy. It's so tedious."

"So you've spoken to other people?"

"As I told you. When necessary."

"Why is it necessary now?"

The bird shook her head and flew away again. Such impatience! Ava would have to be careful. Maybe not ask so many questions.

Ava sat quietly while the bird ate the bread.

"All right, then," said the bird. "You may now ask for three wishes."

"I knew it! You're enchanted, and this is your punishment! You're a princess or something, horribly trapped in a tiny bird's body!"

"I am *not*."

Ava had ruffled her feathers, so to speak. "I didn't mean *trapped*."

"Never mind. Let's move on."

Three wishes. But she had only one. "Could you—"

"*No.*"

"But I miss him so much."

The bird said nothing.

Ava thought awhile, but not for too long, given the bird's extreme lack of patience. "I wish I had my old room back, the way it was. I hate what my stepmother's done to it—it's like something in a magazine, all fancy and frilly."

"Have you told her that you don't like your new room?"

Ava shrugged. "Not exactly."

"Never mind. Tomorrow you shall have your wish." With that, the bird flew off.

When Ava got home from school the next day, she couldn't believe it. Her room was her room again! There was a blue cotton blanket, almost identical to the one her stepmother had gotten rid of, and plain curtains fluttering in the window, and even the horrible paisley wallpaper had been papered over—with a lovely design, clouds and blue sky.

At dinner, she didn't say a word.

"I don't know what possessed me," her stepmother said, as if Ava had asked. "I had so many things to do today, and instead I changed your room all around, back to the way it used to be. Do you like it?"

Ava nodded.

Ava couldn't wait to tell the bird all about her room, but of course the bird knew. "Thank you, thank you," she said. "It's perfect!"

"Don't thank me. I wasn't the one who stood on stepladders and put up new wallpaper."

"But—"

"Next wish," the bird said.

She didn't have one ready. Her new room, and how happy and comfortable she felt in it, had occupied all her thoughts. She had to think. . . . "I hate all the clothes my stepmother bought—slinky pants with shiny studs, suede shirts with fringes, hair barrettes that weigh about ten pounds. I wish I had my old stuff back."

"Have you told her you don't like these new things?"

Ava shrugged. "Not exactly."

"Never mind. Tomorrow you shall have your wish."

Ava, home from school, rushed to her closet. Amazing! These were clothes she would have bought for herself—they were her taste *exactly*. Flannel shirts, sweatshirts, T-shirts, pants with deep pockets.

"It happened again," her stepmother said at dinner. "I had so much to do, but I didn't do any of it. Instead I donated all your clothes to charity and bought you new clothes, like what you used to wear. Do you like them?"

Ava nodded.

"I suppose . . . Well. My mother was always buying my clothes, arranging my room. She said she knew better than I did what a young lady needed. It never occurred to me to question her, so when it came to you . . . Well. I just assumed. But, after all, they're your clothes, and it's your room, isn't it?"

She nodded again.

In the attic Ava couldn't wait to tell the bird how pleased she was. "Thank you, thank you!" she gushed.

"Don't thank me. I wasn't the one who stood on long lines to buy you all those new things."

"But—"

"Last wish," the bird said.

Again Ava didn't have one ready. She had to think. "I wish . . . I wish I had someone to talk to!"

"Tomorrow you shall have your wish."

Ava couldn't sleep that night. What would the bird

come up with? Maybe a new student would show up at school. She would sit next to Ava, of course, and they would hit it off right away. Or maybe one of the girls already at school would decide, out of the blue, to become her best friend. Or maybe the elderly couple in the house next door would move out, and a new family would move in with a girl exactly Ava's age. . . .

None of those things happened.

After school Ava went to the attic with several pieces of bread, but the bird never showed up. She felt cheated. *Three* wishes, the bird had promised! Three, not two!

Ava sulked at dinner.

"What's wrong?" her stepmother asked. "You look upset."

Ava said nothing.

That night she lay on her bed. Even in the darkness, something shiny caught her eye. There was something on top of her bureau, something that hadn't been there before. She got up. It was . . . a hairbrush. With a large silver handle. She ran her fingers over the bristles—not too stiff, not too soft. Exactly right.

She went downstairs and stood right in front of her stepmother, who was on the living room couch, reading.

"Did you get this for me?"

"Oh! Oh! You scared me half to death!" Her stepmother took several deep breaths. "Oh. That's better. Honestly, Ava, it was so quiet, and you haven't said a word in so long—" She looked at what Ava had in her hand. "Well. That hairbrush. It belonged to my mother. I thought . . . I don't know what I thought. I just saw it, and the next thing you know I put it in your room."

"It's wonderful," Ava said.

Her stepmother watched as Ava pulled an elastic band out of her hair. Ava had thick, gleaming, golden hair that covered her like a blanket. "Oh, Ava. You've let your hair down."

"Could you brush it?"

Her stepmother stood behind her and brushed—not too rough, not too light. Exactly right. And as she brushed, Ava talked and talked—the words spilled out of her. Her stepmother didn't say much. But Ava could tell she was listening with all her heart.

LOIS METZGER admits, "I've always been fascinated by 'Rapunzel.' A wicked witch holds a young girl prisoner at the top of a tower. To get to the girl, the witch calls out, 'Rapunzel, Rapunzel, let down your hair!' The lonely, unhappy girl lets her long hair spill out a tiny window and down the length of the tower, and the witch climbs up. In the story for this book, a lonely, unhappy girl is also hidden away—inside herself. But, unlike Rapunzel, when this girl finally lets her hair down, so to speak, she frees herself."

LOIS METZGER has written many short stories and several novels for young adults, including the award-winning *Missing Girls*. She lives in New York City with her husband, the writer Tony Hiss, and their son, Jacob.

THE HARP THAT SANG

BY GREGORY FROST

It was Karla's idea to play on the riverbanks, and Beatrice, who would have preferred to stay indoors that gloomy day, suspected nothing. They played at being pirates. Humoring her younger sister, Beatrice asked what treasure they would seek, and raven haired Karla produced a rag bundle into which she'd put a few trinkets of her own. "You have to put something in too," she urged. Beatrice asked her what, and Karla pointed to the golden bracelet on her wrist. Beatrice clamped her hand upon it, reluctant to part with it. Her father had given it to her for her fourteenth birthday. But Karla said, "It's only for the game, Bea. It's only for a while. It isn't as if we're *throwing* it in the water."

Finally the bracelet went into the bundle.

They set out alone because the river wasn't terribly far from home, and because they were pirates and didn't need to share their schemes with adults. There had been a lot of rain, and the river was high and fast, dark and swirling.

Karla urged Beatrice to follow her, persuaded her to walk along the sharpest bank, above the angry river, to hide the treasure bundle. Then at the last moment Karla seemed to change her mind. She turned back. For a moment they stood almost nose to nose, and Beatrice saw her fate in her sister's eyes. Then Karla pushed her off the bank.

Beatrice cried out, and her fingers pinched at the air for something to catch her, but there was nothing, no root or dangling limb where Karla had turned. Beatrice plunged into the angry river.

Her head broke the surface and she spluttered, calling, "Sister, sister, help!" She choked and waved her hands. But the water turned her every which way. It spun her, tumbled her, hauled her against rocks, to which she tried to cling while the torrent tugged her loose.

High above her, Karla watched, so still that she might have been stone, so still that her sister never saw her. She watched as currents dragged Beatrice under, and dark blonde hair fanned out upon the surface. She watched until even the hair was pulled from sight. Then she knelt and opened the bundle. She took out the bracelet. This was her prize. It was the most beautiful thing in the world, and she had it now. She slid it onto her skinny wrist and tied up the bundle again.

By the time she reached the manor, she was hoarse from screaming. Along the way she threw herself into brambles and bushes. The contents of her bundle lay spilled along the path behind her.

Long before she'd crossed the yard, her parents heard the screams and rushed out to meet her. Servants, too— for her father was a great lord, and many people lived and worked on the estate.

Karla babbled her terrible story of her sister's misstep upon the banks that had tumbled her into the river. Most of the household raced to the river. Over the next few days they combed it, dredged it, took their boats miles downstream until the falls there stopped them. Her father didn't sleep in all those days. He stayed out with the boats, calling Beatrice's name until his voice failed him.

No one found her.

Her mother mourned for months, and Karla closed herself up in her room as if sharing the grief, but actually she was admiring the bracelet. Her father, though he mourned too, watched her so oddly then that she knew he must suspect. Outside of her room, she stopped wearing the bracelet. She worked very hard to make sure she gave his suspicions nowhere to take root. A stone—a ceno-taph—was erected in Beatrice's name, and every day Karla took some trinket or flower or scrap of paper and placed it on the stone, creating her own personal memorial.

In time her father's suspicion ebbed. In time the loss of her sister translated into extra attention lavished upon

GREGORY FROST

her. Eventually she placed the golden bracelet upon the memorial stone. She didn't care for it anymore. She wanted something else. The marriage that had been arranged for Beatrice was renegotiated, and Beatrice's husband-to-be was pledged to her. Karla acquired everything of her sister's, and no one was the wiser.

Antonio had no idea where he was going, just that he had a sense he would find what he needed before he was finished. He'd lost sight of the rest of the gypsy camp. There was no path through the woods here, but his feet seemed to know the way. The gusting wind nearly blew his cap off twice.

Before he saw it, he heard the roar of the river ahead, and he emerged from the woods onto a low bank that led down to a mudflat bend. Protruding from the mud were two curved bones—two ribs from a rib cage.

Cautiously Antonio made his way down to the mud. There were a few other bones scattered across it. Old bones, from the look of them. Antonio took off his boots and walked barefoot into the muck.

Then it was as if the noise of the river faded away. The bones seemed to sing. Awestruck, he listened. The wind gusted and the bones sang again, a high but mournful note. The bones were small—too small to be a man's rib cage. A fawn's maybe. He crouched beside the ribs, and sunlight glinted on strands of gold so fine that he had to peer closer to see them. They were wrapped around and between the ribs like a spider's web. Here was the source of the odd droning—fine, long strands of golden hair

96

drawn tight like the strings of a harp between the bones, and thrumming in the wind.

So, he thought, this was what I was after.

He dislodged the bones from the muck, then wrapped the silken hair around them. He didn't imagine that the hair and bones belonged together—had ever been part of the same creature—but he was a gypsy, and his world was full of connections and coincidences.

It was a year later that Antonio was invited to perform for a wedding banquet. He had long since finished his remarkable harp made from the beautiful bones, polished and carved with triskeles and small figures. The golden angel hair—and he had come to think of it as strands from an angel's head—he had wrapped tightly around the pegged strings to make them glint; he couldn't say just why. It wasn't the sort of thing one did with a harp, but some instinct had guided him, and the music those strings made was sweeter than that of any other instrument he'd ever built, sweeter than any his companions or anyone else had ever heard. That was how word reached the household of the lord who was throwing a banquet for the wedding of his daughter, and how Antonio, a distrusted gypsy, was offered a handsome fee to make sweet music before and after the ceremony.

He drove his wagon to the estate, accompanied by other musicians from his camp who would play krumhorn and bodhran beside him. It was the gypsy way: Good fortune was shared.

The banquet hall was spectacularly prepared, with flags and streamers all lavender, pink, and white. Rose petals were sprinkled across the floor, and sunlight cascaded in through the leaded glass windows. The musicians sat at the rear of the hall, in a boxed area to the left of the aisle where the bride would come walking. The crowd milled about, and everybody was finely dressed. They chatted and laughed, warming to the celebration. Yet when Antonio began to play, those nearest him stopped whatever they were doing and listened. Even the servants forgot themselves momentarily, in thrall to his music. His harp made it seem as if heaven itself had entered the hall.

Then he began a gentle lullaby. His companions exchanged glances, and Antonio himself seemed bemused by the tune his fingers were forging, as though they played without his command. He glimpsed a woman rising at the other end of the hall, turning, her face alarmed. The lord of the manor hurried to her and from her to Antonio, waving his hands. "Please, not that song," he insisted. Antonio made himself stop, though his fingers seemed almost to want to continue. He had to curl them into fists. "That was a song our long-dead daughter used to sing," the lord went on, "and while you've no way of knowing, it grieves my wife to hear it now. Especially on this occasion."

Antonio nodded. "Forgive me, sir, for in truth, it's not even a song I know." He set down the harp.

"Not a song you know?" asked the lord. "But then, how did you perform it?"

"I can't say, my lord. It was as if the tune were coming from the harp to me instead of the other way about." Folding his hands, he asked the others to play awhile without him, then sat most humbly in the hope that his lordship wouldn't require a more sensible explanation since he had none to offer.

Fortunately for Antonio, the time had come for the lord to retrieve his daughter. He departed from the chamber, and upon that cue people began to line up on either side of the aisle. More flower petals were sprinkled down the middle of it, and a white sash was tied across it at the far end. On the opposite side of the sash, the groom awaited, looking bold and merry, smiling to his friends and well-wishers.

The doors beside the musicians opened. The lord entered the room in a solemn promenade. Beside him his daughter, Karla, clasped his arm. She glanced at Antonio, and the bright excitement on her face clouded, though he could not imagine why. He had never set eyes on her before that moment. She reached up and pulled the white veil over her face.

Even as she hid her unease, the harp at his side began to vibrate, and the plangent music of its gilded strings formed into words that called out, "Oh, sister!"

Karla gasped and took a step away, pushing against her father. She stared into Antonio's eyes, and while his remained an expression of complete innocence, hers were one of horror-fueled guilt. She found her father's gaze sharp-edged with suspicion. Only the veil safeguarded her.

He took her arm again. "Come," he said, and led her forward.

On her first step, the harp's strings sang again: "Oh, sister, how could you treat me so!"

Crying out, Karla tore free of her father's guiding arm. She backed away, but the doors had been closed after her. She pressed against them as if she might melt between the panels.

At the far end of the hall the woman who'd become animated by Antonio's earlier performance now started up the aisle. "Beatrice," she called. "Beatrice?"

The harp sang, "Mama!" and the woman stopped, her hand pressed to her mouth. The young groom followed with uncertain steps behind her.

The lord and the gypsy both stared in wonder at the harp. Their eyes met, and each shared in a realization of what was transpiring here.

Her father returned to Karla. "We must continue down the aisle or give up the marriage," he said. "You know you don't want to do that." She, half mad, could not think how to deny him without confessing everything. His hand closed about her arm, and like a force of nature he walked her forward again. She stiffened as they came abreast of Antonio, but her father drew her on.

"Oh, sister," cried the harp, "envious sister, who drowned me for my bracelet and my place."

Karla wailed, "No, no!" but her father would not let her go this time.

"Sister!" cried the harp.

Karla collapsed at her father's feet. He dropped her arm and looked down upon her.

The harp ceased to speak, but invisible fingers played the lullaby that Antonio had been forbidden to perform. Like a small child, Karla clutched her father and begged, "Forgive me, please!" He stood, unmoved. She lowered her face and drew her arms over her head, as if the gown and veil might swallow her up.

The harp strings fell silent. "Forgive me, sister." Karla sobbed into her skirts, but the harp didn't reply.

His wife came forward as if to comfort the girl, but the lord ordered, "Leave her be." He stared darkly upon her. "I don't know what we'll do now, but love her we dare not. On the day she committed it, I suspected her crime. I saw her sister's bracelet upon her wrist, but I didn't want to acknowledge it. I feared to lose both my children, while this cold and witchy creature set about playacting the mourning sister to misdirect the doubt I had. She's as human as a watch spring. There's nothing she could say to me now that I could ever trust not to be the mechanism's cunning to gull us more." To the groom he remarked, "You're fortunate it was today this harp found its way here." He glanced darkly at Antonio, then took his wife by the arm and left the hall. She seemed ready to collapse as Karla had, but he would not let her, not yet.

The guests were left to wonder, to gossip and surmise. The family of the dazed groom surrounded him and drew him away, and quickly the others followed. They swirled around Karla like water around a rock, never saying a word to her. Soon the hall was empty. When Karla raised her head again, even the musicians had departed and the candles had been snuffed. But the lullaby played through the hall.

Karla got to her feet. The harp was gone. How did she still hear it? She covered her ears and fled the room, but the lullaby followed her into the hall. She ran from the house. The song pursued her there, too. Wedding guests saw her race across the yard and out a side gate.

In the woods the song clung to her. She pounded at her head to drive it out. The voice of the harp called, "Sister, sister, how could you kill me?"

She shrieked finally to drown it out but heard Beatrice even above her own screaming—as if Beatrice floated right beside her, lips to her ear. "Sister, sister."

She beat at her head, tore at the veil, at her hair. Her dormant conscience awoke in that voice. She ran blindly as if she could escape herself.

Without realizing, she ran straight off the bank above the river.

The current snatched her. She surfaced, choking, gasping. Her arms flailed for purchase. She struck a rock but was dragged along before she could grab on to it. Thus her sister had gone, and in terror she looked back at the bank, and maybe for a moment there was a figure standing there—she was spun about too fast to be sure. Her white dress billowed on the surface as if to buoy her, but claws of hidden currents grabbed at her legs and dragged her down. In the dark, swirling waters she heard her sister's voice, and she opened her mouth to cry, "Beatrice!"

After that there was only the uninhabited veil upon the surface, floating along like foam.

The lord caught up with Antonio on the road. The gypsy drove the wagon without speaking to his two accompanists. Despite the failure of the wedding, they'd been paid the promised sum for their playing, if grudgingly.

The two had bombarded Antonio with questions: Did the bones of the harp belong to a dead girl? Had he known all along? He told them nothing. The harp that had seemed extraordinary before now seemed to bear a curse.

Then the lord, riding alone, caught up with them, and the two vanished into the wagon and left Antonio to face what they were sure could be only trouble.

"The harp," inquired the lord when he'd dismounted. "Might I see it again?" Antonio turned, and one of his friends handed it to him. He offered it to the man below him.

With trembling fingers, the lord took the harp. He held it by its arms as if wanting at the same time to embrace it and fling it away. Forlornly he said, "She's gone."

"Not gone," replied Antonio. "She's been with you all this time. She was waiting for this day." He didn't know if what he said was true, but he felt it was something this man needed to hear more than truth.

"Would you—would sell this harp?" asked the lord.

"If you desired it, I would, my lord. It has more of your daughter in it than it does of my talent."

The lord nodded. He offered Antonio a large purse. "I don't know how to play it," he said. "Perhaps you could teach me?"

Before Antonio could answer, the lord plucked a string, idly, and the harp sang—not as before with the voice of his lost Beatrice. Now it sang in two distinct tones forming a perfect harmonic interval. Yet he had touched only one string.

Antonio dropped the reins and climbed from the wagon. The harp had never made such a sound under *his* fingers. He peered closely at his handiwork. Then he pointed at it in wonder.

The strings of the purchased harp were bound, each one, in alternating filaments of gold and raven black.

—*For Kayla and Dolly*

GREGORY FROST says, "I love Pentangle. They are one of the great folk music groups, and one of my favorite songs of theirs is a piece called 'Cruel Sister' from an album of the same name. I had been thinking of writing a story from that song for a couple of years, ever since two other writers—Ellen Kushner and Delia Sherman—had invited me to contribute a story to an anthology they wanted to do, in which all the stories would be based on folk ballads. Alas, they didn't get to do it, but they had planted the idea for 'Cruel Sister,' and, thus, by the time Terri and Ellen asked for a story for this anthology, I had already written one in my head. The song ends with the revelations made by the harp, so it was left to me to find a fitting ending for it. I hope I have."

GREGORY FROST is the author of six books and more stories than you can shake a stick at (if that's your idea of a good time). He has contributed to other fairy tale anthologies edited by Ellen Datlow and Terri Windling such as *Snow White, Blood Red* and *Black Swan, White Raven.* His latest novel, *Fitcher's Brides,* is a dark, disturbing fantasy that also comes from a fairy tale—in this case, from the story "Bluebeard." He has been a singer in a garage band, an illustrator, an actor in two dubious horror films, and a researcher for a television series. He promises someday to grow up.

A Life in Miniature

BY BRUCE COVILLE

Once a poor couple worked at a place called TTT, which stood for "Tomorrow's Technologies Today." They swept the labs, cleaned the windows, and generally picked up after the scientists, some of whom were astonishingly messy. The couple lived in a small cottage at the edge of the TTT industrial park and would have been content with their lot were it not for one thing: They did not and could not have a child.

One dark and stormy night there came a knocking at their door. As they rarely had guests, this so frightened the wife that she threw her apron over her face. But the husband scurried to the door. There he found a tall man with fierce eyes, who was much bedraggled with rain and mud.

"My car has broken down," said the man. "May I take shelter here?"

Though he looked like a vagrant, the husband asked him in, partly because he had a kind heart, and partly because he knew security at TTT was such that no outsider could pass its gates.

What he did not know was that their visitor was Dr. Merrill Lyon, head of research at TTT.

After ushering their guest to the table, the husband dialed up some fresh coffee and hot bread, which the table swiftly delivered.

When Dr. Lyon warmed himself a bit, both inside and out, he noticed the wife peering at him from behind her apron.

"Come come, good woman," he said. "You've nothing to fear from me!"

After a bit more coaxing the wife lowered her apron and edged her way to the table. Yet still she seemed sad, and now that Dr. Lyon saw it, he noticed that the husband, too, had eyes weary with sorrow.

"Why such long faces? Is TTT not treating you well?"

"Oh, no!" cried the husband quickly. "We love our jobs!"

This was not entirely true but was probably the wisest thing to say under the circumstances since he could not be sure that their guest had not been sent to spy on them. "It's just that . . ."

When his voice trailed off, his wife jumped in with a vigor that belied her previous timidness. "It's just that we want a little baby boy, sir, and can't seem to have one. Oh, I want a child so much I wouldn't mind if he were no bigger than a mouse."

And that was how the whole thing started.

In his office the next day Dr. Lyon could not stop thinking about the wife's words, which almost seemed an invitation to test a bit of technology he had been tinkering with. Two days later he invited the couple to his lab, where they signed several release forms freeing TTT from all responsibility, then underwent numerous tests and injections.

Not many months after, the wife gave birth to a perfect baby boy. Well, perfect in all ways save one: He was barely the size of his father's thumb! Despite her comment to Dr. Lyon the mother was not entirely happy with this. On the other hand, the tiny infant was so dear that her whole heart went out to him the first instant she saw him.

Word of the miraculous child quickly made the rounds at TTT. Before long many scientists had come to visit the baby, who Dr. Lyon dubbed "Tom Thumb." (Though Tom's parents were not entirely happy with this name, they preferred it to Dr. Lyon's first suggestion: "The Spacesaver 3000, Mark I.")

Eventually even the daughter of the man who owned TTT came to visit. The girl, Titania by name and but four years old herself, was immediately smitten with the baby. "Oh, the dear thing!" she cried. "Please, can I hold him?"

Tom's mother, being no fool, passed the child to

Titania, who cradled him in the palm of her hand and wept bitterly when it was time for her to leave.

The next day came a knock at the cottage door. Before either man or wife had a chance to answer, in swept the little princess (for that was what the people at TTT called Titania), bearing an armload of gifts for Tom.

From that moment on the baby wanted for nothing in the line of clothing, as it was Titania's delight to dress him as if he were a doll. So it was that the child of the humble cottagers wore silks and satins and shoes made of the finest Italian leather—though it must be said that their cost was all in the workmanship, since an entire wardrobe for the lad could be made from a mere handful of scraps. Titania came to visit often and adored the tiny baby, though it did distress her that she often found him scrabbling around on the floor with the mice, who seemed to look on him as a special friend. Tom even trained one to carry him about on its back, as if it were a tiny horse. He named it "Charger," and the two made quite a sight.

Though he grew no taller, Tom seemed to mature rapidly, and when he was but a year old it was decided that he should join the children of the other TTT employees at their day care.

This did not turn out to be an entirely good idea, for he was constantly in danger of being stepped on by the other children. Moreover, Tom himself was the soul of mischief and loved nothing more than to slip into some child's pita bread then stick his head out from behind a cherry tomato and shout "Boo!" just before the poor thing took a bite. These antics led to more than one case of hysteria, several parental complaints, and two lawsuits. Finally the vice president in charge of employee relations decreed Tom would have to be schooled elsewhere.

When Dr. Lyon learned of the problem, he invited the wee lad to come live in the lab. Tom's parents were reluctant to let their boy go, but the doctor made so many promises about the fine education he would receive and the splendid people he would meet that finally, with heavy hearts, they agreed. Tom agreed too, though he insisted that Charger be allowed to come along with him.

Dr. Lyon had a dollhouse custom made for Tom to live in. Though he mentioned it to no one, he also had the dollhouse fitted with cameras and microphones so he could monitor Tom's life.

Tom loved being in the lab, for all the scientists who came through would stop to talk to him and compliment him on what a fine lad he was becoming. In fact, by the time he was four Tom had the wits and skills of a ten-year-old. Dr. Lyon made many notes questioning whether this was a function of his reduced size.

Tom was enormously curious, and he and Charger were always prowling the lab to see what Dr. Lyon was up to. Finally the scientist ordered Tom to stay on the table-tops, saying he was afraid someone would step on the tiny boy if he was running loose on the floor. This so frustrated Tom, who now could not get from one table to another without being carried, that one of the TTT engineers created a system of towers and bridges for him. Soon every lab table had a five foot tower at each end, each tower being connected by a narrow bridge to the one at the next table, with the bridges sufficiently high that the scientists could walk below them with no problem. The kindly engineer added a system of pulleys so all Tom had to do was climb into a little cup and then hoist himself to the top of the towers.

Now he could travel freely about the lab and was much happier. Most of the scientists soon became used to the sight of the thumb-sized boy scampering about overhead. Dr. Lyon, however, seemed to be somewhat nervous about having Tom move around so easily. And after a while Tom noticed that every night the doctor carefully locked his center desk drawer. The boy wondered what was in the drawer that Dr. Lyon hid it so carefully, but as the man always took the key with him, he was not able to find out.

The lab was a place of great fascination for Tom. He loved the bubbling test tubes and the crackling power sources and the strange-smelling concoctions so much that even though Dr. Lyon repeatedly begged him to be careful around them, he could not resist getting too close—which was how he happened to tumble into a small pot of something extremely disgusting one afternoon.

The goo, as it turned out, wasn't an experiment at all, but something one of the lab assistants had been cooking for lunch that had been left on the burner too long and gone bad.

Tom thrashed and struggled to get out, but the gluey stuff held him fast. Even when the lab assistant picked up the pot and scraped it into the garbage, Tom wasn't able to make himself heard above the deafening music that the assistant was playing while Dr. Lyon was out of the office.

When the lid of the garbage can closed over Tom, he was sure his end had come. The darkness was so complete it was as if he had been swallowed, the papers in the can stuck to him when he tried to move, and every time he struggled too vigorously, he sank deeper into the trash. Twice someone opened the can to throw something in, but by that time Tom had sunk so far that the papers above him muffled his tiny cries.

He wept bitterly.

Finally the lid was lifted again—and stayed open. For a brief moment Tom thought he would be saved. But swift hands tied the top of the plastic bag lining the can, sealing Tom in. He felt the bag being taken from the can and cried out more desperately than ever. Alas, his voice was muffled by the jumble of trash. The bag was flung somewhere, moved, flung again, and Tom was certain he would soon run out of air or be crushed or something equally terrible. But he was not the sort to despair. With his tiny fingers he began to claw at the plastic that held him in. It was maddening work, for the plastic slipped and slid, but he finally managed to tear open a small hole. Thrusting his hand through, he waved it about, hoping someone would see him.

Someone did—an old seagull who was scanning the

trash heap for something interesting. Landing on the bag, the gull quickly pecked it open and snatched Tom up. Off it flew, Tom dangling from its beak.

The boy struggled and squirmed until he realized that if he *did* manage to get the bird to let go of him, he would be dashed to his death on the rocks below. What a choice: be eaten by a bird, or plummet to a stony death!

But when the gull flew out over some water, Tom quickly swung his legs up, wrapped them around the gull's neck, and began to squeeze. The startled bird opened its mouth to squawk. Tom immediately released his legs and fell to the water some thirty feet below. He struck hard and was stunned for a moment. He began to sink. But before he had a chance to worry about drowning, an enormous pike struck, swallowing him in one gulp—which was actually lucky for Tom, as it saved him from being slashed to bits by the pike's needle-sharp teeth.

Down the gullet Tom slid until he was in the fish's stomach, which burned him like fire.

This time he was sure he had come to his final moments. But as he was waiting for his doom, he felt the great fish jerk and convulse. It was flung around then smacked down, moving so violently that Tom had no idea what was happening at all—until he saw a smear of light. He began to shout and scream and thrash about himself.

"Well, well, what have we here?" cried a rough voice. "Something the fishie et is still alive. Let's have a look, shall we, missy? Always interesting to see what these beasties swallow down."

Tom shrank back as a flash of silver cut open the stomach wall. He covered his eyes to shield them from the bright light that flooded in. Then he felt himself once more plucked up.

"It's Tom!" screamed a familiar voice. "It's Tom! Oh, do put him down. Please, please be careful!"

A moment later Tom was standing on a table, and little Titania was gently pouring water over him to wash away the many revolting things that had covered him that day. "Poor Tom," she kept saying, and sometimes she would start to cry. "Poor, poor Tom."

"Not so poor," he said. "I'm still alive. But how did I get here?"

"That's what I'd like to know," said a deep voice.

"Who are you?" asked Tom, gazing up at the tall bearded man.

"I'm Titania's father, Arthur Kring. We were out for an afternoon of fishing on Lake TTT, and when we caught a fish we caught you as well. Thank goodness the captain here planned to grill the thing now. But how in heaven's name did you get inside that monster?"

After Tom told them of his adventures, Titania said, "Daddy, we can't let Tom stay in that horrible lab anymore."

Her father agreed (he agreed with almost everything his daughter said), and so Tom was brought to live at the executive quarters of TTT.

He sent for Charger to come live with him, but the mouse had disappeared and had not been seen since the afternoon Tom fell into the pot.

Though Tom mourned for his old friend, all in all his new home was very pleasant. He wanted for nothing at all since Titania doted on his every wish. But in time he began to have a hankering to see his parents and asked over and over if he might visit them. Finally Titania agreed and said that she herself would take him. So one morning the two set out for the little cottage where Tom had spent his earliest days. To Tom's surprise, he found his father in a state of gloom, and his mother in even greater despair.

"What is wrong, what is wrong?" he asked.

"We've been let go!" wailed his mother, throwing her apron over her face. "After all these years, we've been let go! They're going to replace us with those mechanical men Dr. Lyon invented. Oh, whatever will we do? Whatever will we do?"

"I shall talk to my father," said Titania decisively.

But now the little princess discovered the boundaries of her power, for Mr. Kring told her this was a matter of business, and in those things she must not interfere.

Titania was so vexed she stamped her foot, but it did her no good.

"I'm sorry, Tom," she said sadly. "I cannot help you."

"Perhaps you still can," said Tom. "There is a desk drawer in Dr. Lyon's office that I would like to examine."

"Why?" asked Titania, wiping away her tears.

"I'm not sure. But he was always so careful to keep it locked that it makes me wonder what is in it. Can you help me check?"

"I'll be glad to."

They decided that Titania would visit the lab with Tom hidden in her pocket. While there she would get Dr. Lyon to show her something on the far side of the lab. She would slip Tom out of her pocket, and he would make his way into the desk drawer to see what it contained.

"Why, Titania, what a pleasant surprise!" cried Dr. Lyon when the little princess entered the lab the next day. "We've missed you around here." He scowled slightly at her then added in mock seriousness, "I'm not sure we can forgive you for taking our little friend away from us."

"He's much safer where he is now, Dr. Lyon," said Titania. At the moment this was quite true since he was clutched in her hand, which was in her pocket.

With her other hand she pointed to the far side of the lab. "What's *that*?" she asked, feigning great interest.

Dr. Lyon, well aware that it was important to keep the boss's daughter happy, agreed to explain it to her. As he turned to lead the way, she deposited Tom onto the desk. Quickly he slipped into the center drawer.

In his hand he carried a tiny flashlight that Titania had had made for him. Shining it around him, Tom saw that the drawer was like a long, low chamber, one in which he could stand with his head just barely below the ceiling. To his right he saw an eraser big enough for him to sit on. Behind him were pencils as thick as his legs. Not far in front of him lay a file folder that would have made a nice tennis court for someone his size.

Tom made his way to the top of the folder.

"Spacesaver 3000, Mark I," read the label.

The words had a familiar ring, though Tom could not say why.

He lifted the edge, crawled under it, and began to read. Soon his tiny heart was pounding with rage and excitement.

Suddenly he heard footsteps. Titania and Dr. Lyon were coming back. "Wait, wait," he heard Titania say. "I want you to explain *that* to me."

"In just a moment, my dear," said the doctor.

Stepping behind the desk, he slammed the drawer shut.

Tom was trapped inside! His excitement turned to fear. Had Dr. Lyon known he was in here? Was he trying to catch him? Even if he wasn't, Tom didn't want to be found inside the drawer—especially not after reading what was in that folder.

Clenching his tiny flashlight in his trembling hands, he made his way to the back of the drawer.

It was sealed tight. He should have expected that; there was no way that Dr. Lyon would have a cheaply made desk. He was trapped.

Hours passed. Tom wondered if he would ever get out. Then he remembered that it was Friday. What if Dr. Lyon left for the weekend? Tom began to wonder if he would die from lack of food or water before the drawer was opened again.

Then, to make things worse, his flashlight went out, leaving him in utter blackness.

It was impossible to know how much time had gone by before he heard a scratching at the back of the drawer. New fear clutched Tom's heart. Was something trying to get in here with him? *Scratch. Scratch, scratch.* something was gnawing at the wood. The sound went on and on until Tom thought he would go mad with terror.

Then it stopped, and he heard a new sound, at first terrifying and then, when he recognized it, soothing. It was the sound of a mouse—and not just any mouse. It was his old friend, Charger.

A moment later Tom felt Charger's furry body rub against him. When he grasped his former steed by the tail, it led him to the back of the drawer where it had gnawed a hole just big enough for a mouse, or a boy the size of a thumb, to escape.

"Wait," murmured Tom. "Wait!"

He returned to the folder and with great effort rolled a piece of paper until it was no thicker than a pencil. He carried it to the hole and pushed it through ahead of him. Then he followed Charger through the hole.

The climb to the floor was treacherous, and Tom nearly fell more than once. When at last he was down, he embraced Charger. With the paper underneath his arm, he went back to the dollhouse where he had once lived, which was still tucked into a corner of the lab, and called Titania.

A few minutes later she arrived, guards in tow.

When Tom showed her the paper he had found in Dr. Lyon's drawer, her eyes narrowed in anger.

"Wait until I show this to Father!" she said.

Her father was angry too, not only at Dr. Lyon, but at the jury that awarded Tom half ownership of TTT in compensation for the company's unethical act of combining mouse genes with his own in order to make him come out so small. Dr. Lyons's plea that he was only trying to help humanity overcome its crowded condition fell on deaf ears.

It took several years, but the technicians at TTT finally managed to find a way to make Tom grow to a full two feet in height. At Titania's request they also found a way to shrink her to almost the same size.

Soon after, the pair were wed in a pavilion in front of the very lake where Tom had been swallowed by the pike. His parents sat in the front row, weeping and smiling, and cheered when the happy couple kissed.

As for Tom and Titania Thumb, they ran TTT wisely and well, doing much good in the world and turning a tidy profit as they did.

It was a short life, but a happy one.

"When I was eight or nine," says BRUCE COVILLE, "my cousin gave me a huge volume of fairy tales as a birthday gift. I doubt there was any book in my childhood that I turned to more often, or pored over more thoroughly, than that one. The mysterious quality of the tales it held was endlessly appealing to me, and thinking of it even now, I can feel myself drifting halfway into that other world it spoke of.

"I decided to work with Tom Thumb for this collection partly because I have always been fascinated by great variations in size. The very first book I published was called *The Foolish Giant,* and I have often written about characters who shrink—or were tiny to begin with.

"I suspect such tales appeal to kids because we all start out trapped in a world of giants. What is life for a character like Tom Thumb but an exaggerated version of what all of us experience as kids, when we find ourselves trapped in a world designed for people more than twice our size?"

BRUCE COVILLE was born and raised in upstate New York, where he still makes his home. He has published more than eighty books, including the best-sellers *My Teacher Is an Alien* and *Into the Land of the Unicorns.* Before becoming a full-time writer, he worked as a toy maker, a grave digger, a cookware salesman, an elementary school teacher, and a magazine editor. He is married to illustrator Katherine Coville.

LUPE

BY KATHE KOJA

Ⓠ

Do you ever go into the woods? Not the park, always so dusty-dirty, torn paper wrappers and splintery seesaws, four old trees leaned up like broken boards against the fence. No, I mean the *woods,* the place where the town's noise fades away as if there is no town at all; where the trees stand like an army, where the bears and wild pigs live, and Old Blanca the witch, the place all the grandmammas say *Stay away from!*

In the woods everything is different. The light slants different, like underwater; the grass is sharp and pointy with morning frost. And the smells—a hundred scents, a thousand every second: dead-leaf spice and bitterroot, mold and rot and berry, I couldn't guess or name them all but they don't need names, they just are: like the trees, the needle frost, the slanting light: and me.

In town I have a name—Lupe, for Guadelupe—and a family: Mamma and Papa and Fernando—'Nando, my younger brother. When I want to be mean to him I call him Feonando, because *feo* means "ugly" or "awful." When he wants to be mean to me, he waits till I go to sleep, then puts sweetgum in my hair; it sticks like glue, and the sugar-smell draws the ants. Sometimes I hate 'Nando a lot.

For a while we had another brother, a baby brother: Teodoro. He was tiny and chubby and oh, so soft; it made me happy just to carry him around. I used to put my face in the curve of his neck and breathe in his warm baby smell, then breathe out again in little puffs to tickle him and make him laugh. Mamma said I was like his second mother, Mamma said . . . But then the fever came, like a hot wind blowing over Teodoro, blowing like a desert till he stopped laughing and stopped eating, till finally nothing was left. Mamma let me help her wash him, and dress him in his little white nightgown, and Papa buried him in a dark brown box.

All that night I could hear the wolves out in the forest crying for the moon: It was a sound like the wind, or the moon herself, crying to be so cold and lonely in the sky, like Teodoro crying, all alone in his little brown box. . . . Finally I couldn't help it, I sat up in bed and cried too, so loud that 'Nando woke up and yelled for me to stop. I hit him and he hit me and then Mamma came in, screaming, and hit us both.

Everything changed, after Teodoro died. Mamma was

quiet, not the good quiet that means you're thinking, but the bad quiet that means you can't think at all. She walked around our house like a ghost, hardly eating, never seeming to sleep. Papa just worked, worked, hunched at his bench making figures of mammas and babies, lots of mammas and babies, but all of them sad looking, so sad no one wanted to buy. 'Nando spent all his time at the park, acting foolish, getting into fights. And I went into the woods.

It should have been scary—the long crooked arms of the trees, the rustling leaves whispering behind your back—but I wasn't scared. Maybe I should have been. Maybe I was too sad about Teodoro. Maybe I liked it there. It was quiet in the slant of the sun, and if you sat still, really still for a long time, the animals would come out, the squirrels and the birds and the chipmunks, and rush and eat and play right by you as if you belonged there, as if you were part of the woods too.

But you had to be careful, very careful, not to get too comfortable or feel too safe. Because the big animals, the bears and wild pigs, the wolves were in the woods too, and they knew you didn't belong, some human girl sitting there with bare feet, hair the color of tree bark, it didn't matter to them: they *knew*. They would trample you, or drive you trembling up a tree; the wolves, especially, would eat you up.

That very day I'd seen a wild pig, old boar tusking for acorns, his smell as big as he was: like a hundred old cabbages boiling at once, like something dug up from a year underground. I saw him and he saw me and I ran home as hard as I could, hair flying, breathing through my mouth. When I tumbled inside, 'Nando pinched his nose: "¡Ay di mí! Where you been all day, Lupe, out by the pits?"

Papa stuck his head out from the workroom; his face was powdered with sawdust, a pale brown mask. "The pits! It's nasty there, Lupe. Why in the world—"

"I wasn't by the pits," I said, and pinched 'Nando, a hard twisty nip on his leg. He let out a yelp, danced out of reach and "The woods," he called. "That's where Lupe goes. Carlos and Aimi told me, they said she goes there every day."

Papa came all the way out now, frowning lines in the sawdust mask. In his hand was another mamma-and-baby, just born from the ragged wood. "The woods, Lupe? What do you do there?"

I sit and watch the trees, Papa, and the squirrels dancing like falling leaves. I listen to the sounds that are so small you can hardly hear them. I look for wolf tracks. I drink water from the stream I found. I think of Teodoro. "Nothing," I said.

"Nothing," hollow, like an echo from right behind me, so close I jumped—but it was Mamma, her hair hanging down like black seaweed, her eyes red. "Nothing she does all day, lazy girl. Why don't you help your mamma? Poor Mamma, there's no one for her now."

Papa clutched the mamma-and-baby. 'Nando edged closer to the door. None of us spoke. Mamma squeezed my arm; her hand was damp and hot, as if she had a fever, like Teodoro. "I'll help you," I said. My voice sounded strange, as if I were far away. I wished I were far away, back in the woods, so far inside no one could find me. "What do you want me to do?"

"Go to the woods for me," Mamma said. "Go and see Old Blanca."

Papa's lips went tight; he set the wooden people down. "No, Maria," he said, hands on Mamma's forearms, his face close to hers as if he would kiss her, as if they were alone in the room. "That's no errand for a child. Old Blanca is—"

"A *bruja*!" 'Nando shouted. "She eats children, she's a witch!"

Mamma wrenched away from him, her eyes redder now, an awful red; they made me think of the wild boar, fierce and tusking, blind to everything but hunger. "Who else can help me? Who else will give me back what I have lost?"

"Maria, no! Maria—"

"I'll go," I said; I had to say it twice to make them hear. "I know the way, Mamma, I'll go to Old Blanca for you."

'Nando's eyes were round and bright; Papa's lips parted, but he said nothing. Mamma scrambled to fill a basket, the split-oak basket she used for the market, piling it with tidbits and scraps of shiny cloth, some wheat cakes, a spill of fat purple grapes, the half-made mamma-and-baby, and "You take this," she said to me. "Take it and give it to Old Blanca. She'll know what to do."

"Take this too." Papa held out one of his carving tools,

a wicked little scraping knife with a yellow handle. "Be careful, *querida*," he said into my ear; he had tears in his eyes. "And hurry right back."

The basket was heavy on my arm, as if it were filled with rocks, or bones. I tucked the knife into my skirt pocket and reached for my cloak, but it still had the smell of the boar, rank and fresh, so I took Mamma's instead, long and soft and red. It brushed the ground as I strode toward the woods, the afternoon shadows pointing like fingers back the way I had come, the sun warning me to turn back, but how could I do that? Mamma needed me. And I wasn't afraid, not really. Not of the woods.

I kept a wary eye for that old boar; I was wary anyway, I'd never come here this late before. The trees arched dark above me, like the inside of a church at night. Birds flew, branch to branch, heading for their nests; the squirrels scolded. I stepped rock by rock through the stream, careful to keep Mamma's cloak dry. As the sun dropped lower still, its rays brushed gold through the trees, gleaming gold, like the eyes of wolves.

Old Blanca. *She eats children,* 'Nando had said, which wasn't true, how could it be true? But she did strange things there alone in the woods: dug for bones, brewed roots for poison, built altars of antlers to the harvest moon. People said she could see in the dark; people said she could fly. People said she could change into an animal—an owl, a mule deer, a wolf—any animal, whenever she wanted.

I knew where to find Old Blanca, we all did, knew

enough to stay away. Past the stream there was a clearing where the leaves had been brushed carefully away, the mulch and dirt beat into a ring as if someone had been dancing there, or walking in a circle. And past that, so tumbled down and covered with vines that it seemed like a pile of brush, was the *bruja*'s hut.

With one arm I tugged at the tangled brush, searching for the door; the basket handle dug into my arm as I knocked, one, two, firm with my fist and "Excuse me!" I called—and scared myself, my voice sounded so loud in the quiet. "Excuse me, Grandmother Blanca, I have something for you!"

No answer, only the faraway bird sounds, the brooding quiet of the hut. Something rustled behind me, a stealthy sound. I turned fast, the scraping knife snatched from my pocket—but no one was there.

Heart pounding, I knocked again, more firmly this time. Maybe she was sleeping inside; maybe she had turned herself into a spider with tiny little ears. "*Abuela* Blanca! Please, my mamma needs you!"

Still there was no answer. Perhaps she was not home after all. My shoulders slumped; I thumped the basket down. Now what? Leave it there for the mice to nibble, the raccoons to gnaw to bits? Go home and tell Mamma that I had failed? *Who else can help me? Who else will give me back what I have lost?*

A third time I pounded at the door, hard now, with all my strength. "Let me in! Let me in, *Abuela* Blanca!"

—and just like that, like magic, the door opened,

swinging on its hinges as easily as a breeze. My heart galloped like a racing horse. I took a step, two steps, I was inside.

It was a strange place, but pleasant, as if the woods had come indoors: jumbled, dark, and fragrant, with hanging roots and tumbled apples, big jars of clear stream water, a squat black stove like a little campfire—but no one was there, no one but a skinny white cat curled, half-dozing, by the stove.

"*Abuela* Blanca?" I asked, feeling frightened and foolish and excited all at once: Maybe it was her, maybe she truly could change her shape! But the cat just opened pale eyes at me, and blinked, and yawned—then leaped up, bow-backed and hissing, not at me but at something behind me—

—as the room faded away like a candle snuffed, and I whirled on my heel so fast I dropped the basket, grapes and cakes and wooden people spilling on the floor, the knife again bright in my hand—

—to see a gray wolf, timber wolf, *lobo* with hard yellow eyes. Big, oh he was big, he seemed almost as tall as I was, his great gray haunches and paws, he stared at me and I stared at him, the cat beside me, her puffed-up tail brushing my legs—

—as the wolf lunged forward, so fast I couldn't move, his red jaws open and I think I screamed, a wild wailing little scream and the cat screamed too, a pink shriek as the wolf snatched up in those red jaws the wooden people, mamma-and-baby and *crunch! crunch!* he bit them in two, their bodies falling one way, their sad little heads another, and for some reason this took away all my fear, took it and turned it into rage, the way Old Blanca turned roots into poison, turned herself into birds and beasts and "Stop it!" I cried, and struck at the wolf, drove the knife with all my might—

—but he was gone, disappeared, as if he had never been at all: I stood there trembling so I almost dropped the knife. The room came back to life around me, the crackle of the stove, the cat sniffing my sandals, the smell of the herbs so strong I felt dizzy and had to sit down, right there on the floor beside the cat. "*Abuela* Blanca," I said out loud, although I knew she could not hear. "I'm going now. I'm going to tell my mamma—"

"Tell her what?"

I think I screamed again, a tiny scream; I know I fell over, right on my back like a turtle, staring up from the floor at a tall gray woman in a dirty white dress standing over me, arms crossed; she wasn't smiling.

"What are you going to tell her? That Old Blanca was busy? I *am* busy." She had a voice like two sticks rubbed together, raspy and dry. "Too busy for you, *niña*. Take your clutter and go."

"I brought—I brought you . . ." the basket, where was the basket? But now the grapes were squashed, the wheat cakes scattered, the wooden people ruined—

"Are you looking for this?

Like magic, her hand was under my nose, long hairy fingers holding the mamma-and-baby but somehow—more magic? real magic?—they were whole again, heads and bodies, the mamma with her arms around the baby . . . and they were smiling, both of them, happy carved smiles as "Go home," Old Blanca said. Was she smiling, too? "Go home and tell your mamma to wait for the moon."

Wait for the moon? What could that mean? I got to my feet, took the wooden people, pulled my skirts in a curtsy and "*Gracias,*" I said. "I will tell her." I curtsied again, turned for the door but "You," said Old Blanca, *Abuela* Blanca. "You like the woods, don't you, Lupe?"

Golden eyes like the wolf's, gray hair like the wolf too. "I do," I said; how did she know my name? The cat wound around my legs, sniffed my sandals again. "I come here every day."

"Come back and visit me," she said. There was no mistaking her smile now. She ran one hand across my face lightly, like a breeze, like a brushing leaf, like the tickle of fur; gray fur. "I'll show you some things you'll like to see. . . . But hurry home now," in the first, hard, dry-stick voice. "Your papa is very worried."

"*Gracias,*" I said again, and I did hurry, fast and sure though the woods were pitch-dark, I could barely see my hand before my face—but that didn't seem to matter, I knew where I was going, I never lost my way or stumbled once.

On the path to my house I saw all the lamps were burning. 'Nando was waiting at the door and "Where were you!" he shouted, as if I'd been away a year. "What took so long, what did she say? Is she really a witch?"

I felt in my pocket for the smiling wooden people. "Where's Mamma?" but here came Papa to swoop me up, hug me so hard my breath whistled out, and "Thanks be," he said. "Your mamma is sleeping. . . . What happened out there, Lupe?"

How could I tell him? What should I say? So instead I showed him the smiling mamma-and-baby. He looked at it for a long time, his face still and solemn in the lamplight. Then "It's late," he said. "Time for bed. 'Nando, you too."

❧

Wait for the moon. I never did find out what that meant, but Mamma slept all that night and long into the morning, and when she woke up she was the old Mamma again, talking, eating, no more tears. Her red cloak was dirty-brown at the hem, and black on the back where I'd fallen, but she didn't scold me, or even seem to care. She just added it to her basket of washing and went down to the well.

The wooden people were set up on the table, a little bunch of flowers tucked beside them. Papa started carving lots of smiling mammas-and-babies; people liked them, and bought them, as many as he could carve.

And then one morning Mamma came crying to breakfast, and we all got worried, but she was smiling through her tears and "What do you think?" she said, one hand reaching for Papa's. "We're going to have another baby soon!"

Papa's eyes filled up too, and he kissed Mamma's

hand; 'Nando started hollering about another brother but "The baby's a girl," I said. "Call her Blanca." Everyone looked at me, and I felt my cheeks get pink. Where had the words come from? I didn't know, they just popped out. But I knew I was right.

When I asked *Abuela* Blanca about it later, she smiled and nodded, but didn't explain, just gave me the pestle and mortar and set me to grinding: wild thyme and pepper-grass, bright yellow lupine, while she sat on the stool beside me and braided her long gray hair.

꩜

"'Lupe,'" says *KATHE KOJA*, "is my second retelling of the Red Riding Hood story—the first was in a book of fairy tales for adults—and I find her even more compelling this time around. There's something very brave and cool and mysterious about that girl walking into the dark woods all alone. I wonder if I could do it? Maybe that's why I wrote this story: to take another walk, to test myself again in that dark wood."

꩜

KATHE KOJA is the author of *Straydog* and *Buddha Boy,* as well as several novels for adults. She lives in the Detroit area with her husband, artist Rick Lieder, and her son, Aaron.

AWAKE

BY TANITH LEE

That first night she woke up, which was the night after it had just *happened,* Roisa had been surprised. She'd been upset. She knew something had previously gone terribly wrong—exactly like when you have a bad dream, and you wake and can't remember what it was, only that it was awful, and the *feeling* is still there.

Now, of course, she was used to waking like this. She looked forward to it every night near morning, when she lay down to sleep again.

She sat up, threw back the light embroidered cover, and slipped from the bed. She slept clothed always, in the rose silk dress she had been wearing the evening *It* happened. Yet the silk was always fresh, as if just laundered and pressed smooth by hot stones. She herself was also always fresh, as if just bathed and scented, and her hair washed in the essences of flowers. She had long ago ceased to puzzle over that, though before That Night keeping herself so perfect had been a time-consuming daily task.

Roisa was sixteen. It had been her sixteenth birthday, the day it happened. Now she was still sixteen, but she had done and learned such a lot. She knew that the cleanness, and everything like that, was simply because of Great Magic.

By the bed was a little (magically) new-baked loaf, apples and strawberries (magically) just picked, and a china pot of mint tea, (magically) brewed and poured.

Roisa made her nightly breakfast.

Then she left the attic room.

Outside, the narrow stairway was as it always was, dirty and cobwebbed, thick in dusts. But when the skirt of the silk dress brushed through the muck, nothing stuck to it.

She was used to that also.

As she was to the people standing about lower down, absolutely stone-still, as if playing statues in some game. There were the ladies-in-waiting first, the three who must have meant to follow her up to the attics that evening. Unlike on Roisa, webs and dust *had* gathered on them, spoiling their gorgeous party clothes and jewelry and carefully arranged hair. It was a shame. Roisa still felt sorry for them, if in a rather remote way.

The first time, it had really shocked her. She had shouted at them, pulled at them, tried to make them move. Then, worse than these, the other things—for example, the cat that had become a furry *toy* cat on the lowest landing, the bird that stood on the still with its wings fanned out, never lowering them, never using them to fly off. And the young guardsman she had always liked, standing motionless, already dusty in his splendid uniform, his blue eyes wide open, not seeing her at all.

Worst of everything, however, had been to find her parents—her funny, pretty mother, her important, grand father—sitting there like two waxworks in the carven chairs from which they'd been watching the dancing in the Hall. The dancing from which Roisa had escaped, actually, to meet secretly with the guardsman—but somehow she had missed him—and then—then instead she had, also somehow, gone up into the attics of the palace . . .

Roisa had cried when she woke that first night. She had felt no longer sixteen, but about six. She had put her head into the lap of her mother's dress, clutching her mother's body, which felt like a cold rock. Sobbing.

That was when *They* came.

They—the ones who told her. The ones with the magic.

When she got down to the palace Hall tonight, Roisa did pause, only for a minute or so, to dust her mother.

She always did that. It seemed essential. Because of Roisa's attention to her mother, the Queen still looked glamorous—her hair and necklaces still shone.

The King, Roisa didn't try to dust. She would never

have dared because in the past he had seldom touched her, and then only with the firmest of hands, the coolest of kisses.

Beyond the Hall lay the royal gardens, into which, her dusting done, Roisa ran.

Oh—it was full moon tonight.

Once, wonderful scents had drifted here from lilies and from arbors overgrown by jasmine. A gentle breeze blew this evening, and not one of the now-scentless flowers, not one of the tall, graceful trees stirred. Not a single leaf moved, nor even the wind chimes hung in the branches.

By the fountain—whose jetting water had stopped in a long, faintly luminous arch, like rippled glass—the two white doves sat, as they had done now for years. The doves didn't move. Nothing did. Not even the moon, which lived in the sky—at least, it never did when she saw it. Only the night wind, the breeze, only that ever moved.

Roisa glanced about her, by this time no longer worried over the time-frozen gardens. Not even the fish in the pool, still as golden coins, concerned her anymore. There was nothing she could do about any of this.

Just then something seemed to ride straight out of the moon.

They had come back. As they always did.

With the brilliant flutter of sea spray, thirteen white horses landed on the lawn. On the back of every one sat a slim, clever-faced lady with flowing hair, each of a different color—and these tints ranged between apricot and copper, between jet and mahogany, from flame to pewter to violet. Everything sparkled—horses, ladies—with gems, beads, *fireflies*—Then the thirteenth horse came trotting forward, and the thirteenth rider swung from her gilded saddle, light as air. Even though by now she knew this person so well—better, probably, than she'd known her own mother—Roisa never quite stopped being surprised by her.

She was a Fey, of course. One of the Faery Faer, the Elder Ones.

"Awake, I see," said the Thirteenth Fey, whose name was Carabeau (which meant something like *My-friend-who-is-good-looking-and-has-her-own-household*). "Up with the owl, my Roisa. Come on, let's be off."

So Roisa mounted the horse behind Carabeau, as she always did.

After which the thirteenth horse and all the other twelve horses lifted up again into the sky. They weren't winged, these faery steeds—it was just that they could, when they or their riders wanted, run as easily through the air as over the earth.

In seconds the great palace and its grounds became small, far off and far down. It was possible to see, all round them, the high wall of black thorns that kept out all the world. And beyond the thorn-wall, the deserted town, the deserted weedy fields, and ruined cottages from which everyone had, over the years, dejectedly gone away. For the palace was under a curse that would last a century, and everybody knew it.

❧

Roisa laughed as the horses dived up and up. The moon was like a huge white melon, hung on a vine of milky clouds. The shadows of the horses ran below them over moonlit forests, over looking-glass lakes and gleaming, snake-winding rivers, over sleeping villages and marble cities that had also intended to stay wide awake.

"Look, do you see, Roisa?" asked Carabeau, and she pointed with her long, ringed finger at an open courtyard in one of the cities. There was torchlight there and music and dancing—but all stopped utterly still. Exactly like the scene in the palace they had left behind.

"Do you see the banners?" asked Carabeau. "The lights and the colored windows. Look at the girls' rich dresses and the fine clothes of the men. Look at that little dog dancing."

And the little dog *was* dancing, up on its hind legs, cute as anything. Only right now it didn't *move*.

Roisa sighed.

"What, my dear?" asked the Faery.

"I wish—" said Roisa.

"Yes? You know you can say to me or ask me anything, my love."

"Yes, I know. I'm only—sorry I can't ever see—what it's *really* like—I miss it, Carabeau. Only a little bit. But I do."

"Your old life, do you mean? Before you fell asleep and then woke up with us."

"Yes."

"Before the Spinning Wheel and the Spindle with its pointed tip."

"Yes. Oh—it's marvelous to fly about like this, to see everything, and all the foreign lands—the towers and spires so high up, the splendid rooms, the mountains and seas—I remember that forest with tigers, and the procession with colored smokes and elephants—and the great gray whale in the ocean, and the lighthouse that was built before I was even born—"

"And the libraries of books," said Carabeau softly, "the treasure-houses of diamonds, the cathedrals, and the huts."

"Yes," said Roisa.

She hadn't known before she began that she would say any of this. She hadn't known she *felt* any of it. (Nor did she think if Carabeau might be testing her in order that she be sure of this very thing.)

"Is it because," said Carabeau, "when you visit these sights with us, time has always stopped?"

"Yes—no—"

"Because, Roisa, one day that may change. How would that be for you, if the people moved and the clocks ticked?"

"Of course—of *course* I wish everything was like that—so I could see it properly *alive*. But . . . it isn't only that. I want—to live *inside* it—not outside all the time."

"Even if you are outside with us, who love you so well? Even with me?"

"Oh," said Roisa.

Not long after that the horses dipped down. They galloped between scentless streamers of low cloud that should have carried with them the smells of spices or fog or rain. They brushed the unmoving tops of trees with their glittering hoofs and skimmed over a wild night-valley.

This time they landed in the courtyard of a vast old temple. Though some of the building had come down from enormous age, still lines of carved pillars upheld a roof whose tiles, blue as eyes, remained.

In the past they had often come down into the places of human life and walked the horses, or walked on foot, among markets and along busy highways, mingling with the people and the beasts who, "playing statues" like everyone in the palace and everywhere, stayed motionless as granite.

That very first night—so long ago it seemed now—Carabeau and the other twelve Feys had explained to her how, while Roisa and her palace slept their magical sleep, the rest of the world went on about its usual affairs. And how, when she woke up each night, it was inside a timeless zone the Faery Faer could make and carry with them. And then, though she and they might spend all the hours of darkness traveling to the world's four corners and back, no time at all would pass in mortal lands.

"It isn't," Carabeau had said, "that we stop their time—only that we move aside from the time they keep. For them less than the splinter of a single second goes by—for us it is a night."

"But the *wind* moves—" Roisa had cried.

"That wind that blows is not a wind of the world, nor subject to the laws of the earth. That wind is magical, and its own master. But the moon doesn't move, and the sea doesn't. The clouds don't move at all."

Astonished, Roisa had never really understood, which she saw now. She'd only accepted it all.

Of course she had. Thirteen Faeries had told it to her.

Only one thing. That first night she had asked if the other people in the palace—her parents, the guardsman—if they could wake up too, as she had done. Because, as she knew, now the curse had fallen they, like her, were meant to sleep for a hundred years.

"They won't wake," said Carabeau. "Not until the proper hour. Or else there would be no point to any of this."

Tonight they dismounted from the horses in the ancient temple courtyard. It was full of the (magically raised) perfume of myrtle bushes, which had once grown there. Faery lamps of silvery amber and cat's-eye green hung from spider silks or floated in the air. An orchestra of toads and night crickets made strange, rhythmic music. Invisible servants came to wait on the Thirteen Feys and Roisa, bringing a delicate feast of beautiful, unguessable foods and drinks.

They picnicked while the temple bats, caught in that second's splintering, hung above like an ebony garland thrown at the moon.

Roisa once more sighed. She'd tried hard not to.

Carabeau looked into her eyes. But the eyes of a Fey, even if you look directly into them, *can't* be seen into.

"Do you recall, Roisa, what happened that evening when you were sixteen? Then tell it again."

So Roisa told Carabeau and the others what they all knew so well. They listened gravely, their chins on their hands or their hands lightly folded on the glimmering goblets. As if they had never heard any of it before.

But this story was famous in many places.

At Roisa's birth twelve of the Faery kind had come to bless the child with gifts. These gifts were just the sort of thing a princess would be expected to have and to display. So they made her Lovely, Charming, Graceful, Intelligent, Artistic, Well Mannered, Dutiful, Affectionate, Patient, Brave, Calm, and Modest.

But all the while they were giving her these suitable gifts, the Twelve Feys were restless, especially the two that had to give the baby the blessings of good manners and dutifulness, and the other Faery who had to make her modest.

Every so often, one or several of them would steal closer and stare in at the cradle. The court believed they were just admiring the baby. Of course she was exceptional—she was the king's daughter.

Eventually the Feys left the room, leaving it loud with congratulatory rejoicing. By magical means they'd called to their own queen, the Thirteenth Fey, whose name was Carabeau.

Now this was unusual. And in the town, which then thrived at the palace's foot, people looked up astounded to see the Queen Fey ride over the sky in her emerald carriage drawn by lynxes.

When she entered the King's Hall, courtiers and

nobles stood speechless at the honor. But Carabeau looked at them with her serious, wise face, and silence fell. Then she spoke.

"The princess shall be all that's been promised you. You'll be proud of her, and she will fulfill all your wishes. But first she shall have time for herself."

At that a hiss had gone up like steam from a hot stone over which has been flung some cold water.

The king frowned. His royal lips parted.

Carabeau lifted her hand, and the king closed his mouth.

"The Spinning Wheel of Time shall stop," said Carabeau, "because this child, by then sixteen years old, shall grasp the Spindle that holds the thread time is always weaving. Then she shall gain a hundred years of freedom before she becomes only your daughter, and wife to the prince you approve for her."

The king shouted. It wasn't sensible, but he did.

The rest—was history.

When Roisa finished recounting this, which was all she knew, and all the Feys had told her, Carabeau nodded.

"You remember too that night, and how you went to meet the guardsman—you, always so dutiful, but not then—and somehow you missed him, as we intended, and climbed into the attics, and found me there. And when I offered you the chance of a hundred years of journeys, of adventures—of freedom—you gripped time's Spindle, and the Time Wheel stopped."

"I don't remember that—I never have," said Roisa

doubtfully. "Only—going upstairs, and perhaps finding you. But when I first woke afterward, I was frightened."

"But now you are not. Understand, my love, for you this wasn't a curse or doom. It was my gift, the thirteenth blessing. And anyway, at last the hundred years are at an end. This night is your final one among us. Let me tell you what has been arranged for you when you return to the world. Tomorrow a powerful and handsome prince, even more handsome than the guardsman, will hack a way in through the thorns. He'll climb up through the gardens, the palace, mount the attic stair, wondering at it all. He'll find you asleep, as always you sleep by day. He'll wake you up. You'll fall in love at once, and so will he. Then everyone else will wake. The birds will fly about, the cats will purr, the earth's own wind will make the leaves rustle, the sun and the moon will cross the sky. You will live happily till the end of your days, you and your prince, admired and loved by all. The life that, perhaps, now you long for."

The Thirteenth Fey paused. She waited, looking at Roisa.

Roisa realized that something was expected of her. She didn't know what it was—should she thank the Faeries excessively for all the pleasures and travels, the feasts eaten and sights seen? Or for their care of her, their kindness?

Roisa didn't know that the Thirteenth Faery was actually waiting to see if Roisa would say to her, *But I don't really want that!* For Roisa to burst out that No, no, now the choice was truly hers, really she wanted to stay among the Faery kind. Providing only that they would lift the spell from those left in the palace (as she knew they could), then she would far rather become one of their own—if that were possible (and it was). Even if it lost her a princess's crown and all the rough romance of the human world.

But Roisa, of course, *didn't* want that, did she.

She wanted precisely what she had been supposed to have, before the magic of the Spinning Wheel and the hundred years' waking sleep.

And so, when Carabeau murmured quietly, "Are you glad your century of freedom is over?" Roisa sprang up. She raised her head and her arms to the sky. She crowed, (not modestly or calmly) with delight, imagining the fun, happiness, glory that was coming.

And then, startling herself, she found she was crying. Just like on that first night. Just like then.

And when she looked down again at the Feys, they seemed pale as ghosts, thin as shadows, and pearls spangled their cheeks, for the Faery People can't cry real tears.

Then they kissed her. The last kisses of magic. The next kiss she would know would be a mortal one.

"Shall I remember—any of *this*? she asked as, under the static moon, they rode the sky to her palace.

"Everything."

"Won't anyone . . . be jealous?" asked Roisa.

The Thirteenth Faery said, "You must pretend it was all a dream you had while you slept." And in a voice Roisa never heard, Carabeau added, "And soon, to you, that is all it will be."

TANITH LEE says, "The story of the Sleeping Beauty, along with many fairy tales, has always haunted me. I'd considered if, sleeping, she ever dreamed. It took my husband and partner, John Kaiine, to suggest to me that, more than dreaming, she might actually, unknown to any, be regularly waking up. The idea that the thirteenth Fairy might not be as bad as she'd been painted followed swiftly. To me the result here is rather sad—for the fairies and Roisa. Then again, of course she wants her own life back! What, I wonder, would you or I have chosen?"

TANITH LEE, who lives on the coast of England, has written a number of novels for children and young adults, including *The Dragon Hoard, Princess Hynchatti & Some Other Surprises, Prince on a White Horse, Islands in the Sky, Black Unicorn, Gold Unicorn, Red Unicorn,* and *Law of the Wolf Tower,* first of the Wolf Law trilogy.

INVENTING ALADDIN

BY NEIL GAIMAN

a

In bed with him that night, like every night,
her sister at their feet, she ends her tale,
then waits. Her sister quickly takes her cue
and says, "I cannot sleep. Another, please?"
Scheharazade takes one small nervous breath,
and she begins, "In faraway Peking
there lived a lazy youth with his mama.
His name? Aladdin. His papa was dead. . . ."
She tells them how a dark magician came,
said he's Aladdin's uncle, with a plan.
He took the boy out to a lonely place,
Gave him a ring he said would keep him safe,
down to a cavern filled with precious stones,

"Bring me the lamp!" and when Aladdin does,
in darkness he's abandoned and entombed. . . .

There, now.
    Aladdin locked beneath the earth,
she stops, her husband hooked for one more night.

Next day
She cooks
She feeds her kids
She dreams . . .
Knowing Aladdin's trapped,
and that her tale
has brought her just one day.
What happens now?
She wishes that she knew.

It's only when that evening comes around
and husband says, just as he always says,
"Tomorrow morning, I shall have your head,"
when Dunyazade, her sister, asks, "But please,
what of Aladdin?" Only then, she knows. . . .

And in a cavern hung about with jewels
Aladdin rubs his lamp. The Genie comes.
The story tumbles on. Aladdin gets
the princess and a palace made of pearls.
Watch now, the dark magician's coming back:

"New lamps for old," he's singing in the street.
Just when Aladdin has lost everything,
she stops.
     He'll let her live another night.

Her sister and her husband fall asleep.
She lies awake and stares up in the dark,
playing the variations in her mind:
the ways to give Aladdin back his world,
his palace, his princess, his everything.
And then she sleeps. The tale will need an end,
but now it melts to dreams inside her head.

She wakes
She feeds the kids
She combs her hair
She goes down to the market
Buys some oil . . .
The oil seller pours it out for her,
decanting it
from an enormous jar.
She thinks,
What if you hid a man in there?
She buys some sesame as well that day.

Her sister says, "He hasn't killed you yet."
"Not yet." Unspoken waits the phrase "He will."

In bed she tells them of the magic ring
Aladdin rubs. Slave of the Ring appears . . .
Magician dead, Aladdin saved, she stops.
But once the story's done, the teller's dead,
her only hope's to start another tale.
Scheharazade inspects her store of words;
half-built, half-baked ideas and dreams combine
with jars just big enough to hide a man,
and she thinks, *Open Sesame,* and smiles.
"Now, Ali Baba was a righteous man,
but he was poor . . ." she starts, and she's away,
and so her life is safe for one more night,
until she bores him, or invention fails.

She does not know where any tale waits
before it's told. (No more do I.)
But forty thieves sounds good, so forty
thieves it is. She prays she's bought another
                    clutch of days.

We save our lives in such unlikely ways.

❧

NEIL GAIMAN says, "In *The Arabian Nights,* Scheharazade is married to a king who is going to kill her in the morning. She has her sister join her in the bedroom and ask her for a story—and Scheharazade tells stories of such magic and suspense that the king does not kill her, because then he would never know what happened next. She keeps her stories going for a thousand and one nights, and even manages secretly to give birth to several children before she is finally done and the king changes his mind.

"I have a number of stories to tell this week. No one's going to cut off my head if inspiration fails. At least, I hope they're not. I wish I knew where the inspiration comes from, but I don't, and perhaps it's wisest not to inspect too closely.

"There are two stories from *The Arabian Nights* in the poem: 'Aladdin and His Magic Lamp' and 'Ali Baba and the Forty Thieves.'"

❧

NEIL GAIMAN is the author of the *Sandman* comic book series and the adult novels *Neverwhere, Stardust,* and *American Gods.* His first novel for readers of all ages, *Coraline,* was published in 2002. He has found that so far most of the kids who have read it have enjoyed it as an adventure, while the adults who read it have the kind of nightmares from which they wake up screaming, which proves that there is some kind of justice in the world.

My Swan Sister

BY KATHERINE VAZ

My sister, Rachel, was born wrong. There was a mistake in every cell in her body. She lived for a while in an incubator at St. Vincent's Hospital in New York City and looked so tiny in her glass nest. "She's our little swan," said my mother. Rachel was wild and beautiful and seemed ready to fly away. She stared upward, each of her eyes just one drop of pale blue. "Hello," I whispered. "Don't you want to stay with me?" I was eleven and had been waiting for a sister for a long time. She was rose pink. Her head was like a soap bubble, the kind that has panes the color of a rainbow on it. My father put a toy elephant on the top of the glass, to lasso her with its trunk if she tried to float off before we said good-bye. She was going to leave us very soon.

One night while holding Rachel I saw my uncle Jack tapping on the outside of the window of the intensive care unit. He and my mother had not spoken in years. He walks fast, talks fast, reaches high; my mother is slow. She's a young spirit with no sense of time. Sometimes instead of going to work, she decides to go to Central Park and sketch the trees, and my job is to call the pet store where she's a cashier to say she has the flu. Thin as one of her drawing pencils, she forgets to untangle her short black hair. Humming, staring into space, she escapes in her mind to places I can't always reach, and when my father comes home from working at his fruit stand, he helps me make tomato soup filled with carrot pieces cut into daisies. Mother taught me how to twirl around until I'm too dizzy to stand; she made us both necklaces from chains of paper clips.

Uncle Jack is an old spirit who decided he didn't have the patience for us. But there he was in the hospital with his arms around Mother. Rachel had worked a miracle in summoning him back to us. And suddenly our mother was calm and strong, so the little swan must have performed wonders inside of her as well. Uncle Jack was the one to cry. Mother said only, "She's my joy for as many hours or days as I have her."

"You have me now too," he said.

When Rachel was allowed to come home, I invented a plan. I would show her New York. It was the city of my birth, and my mother's birth, and my father's. If Rachel saw how astonishing it was and how much I loved it, she would decide she could not possibly leave us. We lived in our own small nest on West Eighteenth Street, high enough to see the river turn into melted silver when the sun went down. I held Rachel up to our window and said, "It's so exciting here your heart won't ever stop beating!" The clouds were like white wings drifting along above the wide world, bird-high.

The doctor said it was a fine idea to help Rachel enjoy every single minute. We were given permission to take her out. She had a tube attached from her nose to an oxygen machine that was green and thin and had wheels and a handle so that we could push it around. Mother offered to steer the machine and I could carry Rachel. One bright morning, the light dripping gold, we bundled her in a blanket covered with sailboats and took the elevator down fifteen flights. The first man to fall in love with my sister, other than my father and Uncle Jack, was Rafael, the doorman. "Who is this angel?" he shouted when we crossed the lobby.

He took my sister from me and said, "She's a sweetheart."

"Oh, yes," said Mother, happy as a breeze. "Jessica and I are going to show her the city."

"Will you marry me?" Rafael asked Rachel.

Her face was too weak to smile, but she politely shined some light off her eyes.

We made a strange parade, Mother wheeling the machine and my sister in my arms and the tube connecting her to the canister of air, as we strolled in slow motion down West Eighteenth and stopped at Tillmore Bakery Supplies, with its ballerinas for cakes, candles with sparkles, and sugar roses. She would have no birthdays, but we wanted her to see a giant store that held out the promise of every celebration that anyone could imagine. In the narrow aisles, shoppers stepped aside as I showed Rachel the bins of confetti, party hats (I put one on), and the books on how to make wedding cakes that looked like white temples. I showed her cookie cutters shaped like half-moons and turkeys. Rachel slept. "Please try and pay attention," I said. It was almost like our first sisterly quarrel. Mother giggled and took the party hat off my head and pretended it was a megaphone that she held to her mouth to boom out, "Earth to Rachel!"

My sister perked up and grabbed my finger with her right hand as we went back onto the street. Summer was already tipping toward fall. The leaves were turning their usual fire colors, and they scuttled through the streets until people, or taxis and cars, crushed out all that fire under their feet or tires. Maybe it was Rachel's second miracle (or third, fourth, one hundredth) that when people saw us walking at half-speed with the oxygen machine and my sister attached to it, instead of being in a hurry (like my uncle Jack), they also slowed down and said, "Oh, heavens," or "Oh, my," the way people sound the first time they see a tide pool—how pretty, how easily crushed.

We walked under some scaffolding around a bank. "Look, Jessica! Look, Rachel!" said Mother. A construction worker had taken off his metal hat and was bowing at us.

We turned down Sixth Avenue so that Mother could show Rachel the pet store, Animal Kingdom, where she worked. Chihuahuas jumped at the glass in the window display when I lowered her into view. My sister's legs had no strength, but I felt a tremor in her, telling me that she would kick with pleasure if she could. She had raw, thin skin so much like the flesh of these puppies that they forgave her for being a bird. The pet store smelled of grain, leather, newspaper, and the milky scent of baby animals. My mother introduced Rachel to her boss, Doris, who had red hair that she brushed upward into a flame. She was the person I lied to whenever I called to get my mother out of work, and I often feared that Doris would explode into a torch that would burn its way to the truth.

Instead, Doris gave us a toy cloth mouse with a small bell attached to its collar. I shook it in front of Rachel and her head tilted.

"You taking care of yourself, sweetie?" Doris asked my mother. Doris has a voice like a volcano erupting.

"Rachel is taking care of all of us," said Mother.

We visited Mr. Wing, who runs the stationery store where I buy pens and notebooks for school and fold-out maps of the subway. I call him my "Quarter Friend" because one day I was fumbling with my money, and customers were impatient behind me, but I could not bear to use my special quarters with the mementos of the states on them. Mr. Wing laughed and said, "I'm also a collector."

He likes Georgia with its huge peach, which leaves me no choice but to roll my eyes and say, "But Mr. Wing, how *common!*" He never fails to act like this is the richest joke he's ever heard. He keeps a shrine with joss sticks and oranges on a shelf with a red paper poster of the Double Happiness symbol. "Ask for happiness and also a long life, Jessica. A long life without happiness is useless, and a happy life that isn't long is not good either," he once explained to me.

Today he gave Rachel a red envelope with a dollar in it and said, "For good luck."

Oh, the wonders we took in, my baby sister and Mother and me! We saw fish with open mouths, like trophies, in the window at Balducci's, and the bricks and spires of the old courthouse that makes me think of a palace in Moscow. It's now a library. Rachel whined and fussed; was she sad because she could not read books? Mother said, "I'll take you to the big public library with its stone lions, and Jessica and Father and I will read to you at home." I would take her to art museums and show her Monet, who paints the world as if it's melting. And to gardens with birds-of-paradise, lilies, and other children.

We backtracked to West Fourteenth Street for a surprise visit to Antonio's, my father's store, where he sells fruit, vegetables, bread, and candy. Sometimes in the alley behind, the pale green and yellow wrappings from the apples and pears get loose and fly about. They look like the moltings of canaries. When I handle the fruits there, I imagine them full of bird-singing. I put them to my ear and listen. Today I held one to Rachel's ear; she'd been born knowing the language of the skies.

Father was cutting open a burlap sack of lemons when we walked in, and he stopped and smiled. The world froze. "My girls," he said.

He helped Mother steer the oxygen machine around a stand with a pyramid of red apples. They gleamed. They had white kisses on them from being polished and stacked in the light.

Father said, "Rachel isn't too tired, is she? Are you, dear?"

He wiped his hands on his apron. He is skin and bones, and his hairline is already receding. Even his mustache is thin. He handed me a caramel and suddenly, unwrapping it, I was struck as if I had been sleepwalking through my many foolish days and now I was jolted awake—because all of us were here, my sister fluttering against my chest, my Mother exhausted but at peace. There was sweetness in my mouth. We were surrounded by fruit that could be split open to hear better the birdsongs inside them. My father is quiet (Uncle Jack once said he had no ambition), but on the day of Rachel's great adventure, I put my head to my father's chest and discovered that there was singing, loud birdsong, inside my father, too.

The weather turned colder after that, and we agreed to keep Rachel inside. But I longed for the day to take her out again, and I began to knit a jacket for her. Mother bought me thick yarn, blue and white. I wanted to work small waves of blue into a white background. I sat by

Rachel in her crib and my needles clicked out a little music that made my heart sing. They made a *tap, tap* that lulled her to sleep—but many nights she fussed, and many mornings she awakened short of breath. "That's part of a swan's story, Jessica," said my mother when she saw me worrying. "Swans disappear at night and perform bold deeds and must race back by daylight, panting." Mother taught me a cable stitch, and I kept unraveling my work until it came out just right. I did a front panel, the blue yarn peaking along, and started one of the sleeves—not easy! "You'll be wearing it by Halloween," I told Rachel.

I imagined the night as a swarm of crows biting at her feathers. They must have nipped her without mercy because often at first light she was red and crying. I finished the collar. It was rough, not as smooth as it should have been, but I knew I had to hurry.

We ventured into the city one more time: Uncle Jack called to say that he was getting an award for the best sales of stocks and bonds for his company that year. Invitations engraved in gold arrived, including one for Rachel. And one for me: I ran my fingers along my name, indented on the page: *Jessica*. We took a taxicab because we thought Rachel's life would not be complete without a genuine ride in one. The driver kept saying, "Poor child, poor child," until Mother said, "What are you going on about? Sir? She's off to Wall Street. She's in heaven." Mother was in her black velvet dress, and I wore my cranberry velvet one with a matching sash. Rachel was in green togs that made her skin less yellow.

Uncle Jack was wearing a black suit in a theater-like room. When he saw us, he stopped talking to some people and came to hug us. He took Rachel in his arms and said, "It wouldn't be the same without you here."

We could not stay long because Rachel began to cry again, but Uncle Jack ordered a limousine to take us home. I said, "Rachel! Maybe people will think we're rock stars." I'd brought along my knitting in a brown paper bag because I knew that time was running short. I still needed to fix the hem, and one more sleeve was left to knit.

That night I sat up even though my eyelids kept dropping. I stitched the hem in place. Just as I was starting on the right sleeve, Rachel returned early from her night flight, wailing, and I had to comfort her. Father got up; it was almost his usual time. There's a courtyard below us, and I showed Rachel that pieces of the moon had gotten caught in some of the bramble bushes. Father nursed a cup of coffee and stood with us. The sky flipped stars into his cup, tiny ones, a size that could fit over Rachel's eyes. He said, "It's my favorite time. The night is finishing and the day is starting, and they're both together for a moment, right now. It's like there's no one else awake."

"Almost no one," I said.

"Right," he said. "There's us." It was four in the morning. Rachel screeched worse than ever, and he took her from me to see if he could quiet her. Her screams brought Mother to us. We tried to pat Rachel, sing to her. She hollered, she raised the roof. She hit high notes and then low ones and started in again all over.

"She's in pain," said Mother.

An ambulance took Rachel and Mother to the hospital, and Father and I rode in a police car, but I was frantically knitting. I needed to finish the jacket. Hospital clothing is so horrible and unpretty, and Rachel liked to look nice.

When Father and I got to St. Vincent's, Mother met us in the emergency hallway. She was serene, so I thought Rachel would be fine. I had ten rows started of the last sleeve. I'd been getting the thread wet with sweating. The soles of shoes in the corridors made a squishing sound, and some nurses were laughing and I almost yelled at them to shut up. I was still hearing Rachel's screaming inside me.

"They tried to revive her," said Mother. "But they couldn't."

Her insides were too small and too wrong for her to live.

Father and Mother did not want me to see her, but I said I needed to. I had that jacket to give her.

She was lying alone on a table in a room without much light. A white plastic tube like a pretend cigar was still in her mouth, and Father took it out. He was weeping, but Mother was quiet. I stared into Rachel's blue eyes. They were half-open, looking at me—didn't that mean she was alive? Mother closed them with her finger. That's when I began to cry and bellow. I was going to be sick. I'd failed her. I hadn't taken her to the museum, or the library. I hadn't even finished her autumn jacket.

"Never mind," said Mother. She took the jacket from my hand and threw the ugly white hospital blanket off my sister and dressed her in the white-and-blue knitting. I shrieked enough to shatter walls and take the color out of paint. A sleeve was missing! I hadn't been fast or good enough!

"Let me tell you the last part of Rachel's Story," said Mother. "It goes like this: Everyone knows that swans only sing once, the most stunning song of their lives, but unfortunately, it's right before they die. Remember how she screamed tonight? Well, it's only because we're people and she's a swan that we couldn't tell at first that it was the most beautiful song in the world. And the mistake, the terrible mistake, that most people make when a swan dies is that they wrap it completely up tight. They cover its wings! And so, in the grave, a swan turns into a skeleton of a person, nothing more.

"But Rachel has a wing free. That was very thoughtful of you. Now she gets to fly wherever she wants. You'll have to look carefully; she's blue and white, so she's in the ocean and the sky. She wants to stay with you, and do you know why? Because it was brave of you not to turn away from her. You gave her a full life.

"She went to a place of many parties and a hundred candles. A man asked to marry her! Friends greeted her wherever she went. Like a wise old woman, she soothed me and then won over your uncle Jack. Can you believe he loves us again? That was Rachel's doing. Most people in a long life don't do as much good as she did in thirty days. She made the crowds stop and gape at her: What fame!

She dressed up for fancy financial-street events. The city was at her feet; she was already soaring above it. How can she give that up?"

Uncle Jack came to the funeral at the cemetery, and I thanked him for walking in step with me, gripping my hand, because I kept shutting my eyes not to see the graves.

"She won't be able to breathe in the earth," I said.

He pointed at the sky. "She's everywhere now," he said.

Nowadays the subway rumbles and I think, "Listen, there's life underground." I see a white cloud and it's Rachel's swan-like wing, waving to me. Her blue and white jacket fills the air, but it's her bare wing that I want to touch when my feet feel like stone. I'll have to rethink the idea of Double Happiness: One can have a complete, amazing existence in just a few days, and it's joy as big as creation. Rachel is a generous sister because often, as I walk along, she dips down to let me catch hold of her feathers. I lift my sad face and gaze around. The buildings here, they want more and more of the sky, past the simple blue of it. They wear that blue on their collars and keep on stretching. I want the sky of New York, too, and beyond it. I sprout wings on my back, wings on my ankles. My swan sister, Rachel, whispers, "Hold on tight," and what a shock. What a surprise. I'm the one flying.

KATHERINE VAZ says, "The stories of Hans Christian Andersen have always enchanted me, especially 'The Wild Swans.' Elisa, the heroine, must knit shirts made of nettles to change eleven swans back into her brothers, but she runs out of time and cannot finish one of the sleeves. Her beloved younger brother is restored—except that one of his arms remains a wing. What's so beautiful in that notion is that we might do our best to save or repair our loved ones, but the result isn't always as we want or expect. And somehow that falling-short, that affectionate error, that mistake, that wing, strikes us as even more radiant and powerful because it is a visible mark of how much love we had.

"Rachel was a real little girl who did not live long, but—pretty as a swan, light as a feather—she managed to remind my family that even when time runs short, even when we cannot speak, we can still work wonders."

KATHERINE VAZ is the author of two novels and a collection, *Fado & Other Stories,* which won the 1997 Drue Heinz Literature Prize. She has published stories for children in *A Wolf at the Door* and for young adults in *The Green Man: Tales from the Mythic Forest.*